THE MONSTER STICK

THE MONSTER STICK

& OTHER APPALACHIAN TALL TALES

PAUL & BIL LEPP

AUGUST HOUSE, INC.
ATLANTA

Published 1999 by August House, Inc.,
www.augusthouse.com

Printed in the United States of America
10 9 8 7 6 5 4 3

LIBRARY OF CONGRESS CATALOGING-IN-PUBLICATION DATA

Lepp, Paul, 1961–
    The monster stick : & other Appalachian tall tales / Paul & Bil Lepp.
        p. cm.
    ISBN 0-87483-577-1 (alk. paper)
    1. Appalachian Region—Social life and customs—Fiction.
    2. Tall tales—Appalachian Region. I. Title. II. Lepp, Bil, 1970–

PS3562.E6132 M66 1999
813'.54 21—dc21   99-044301

Project Editor: Joy Freeman
Manuscript Editor: Dawn Drennan
Cover and Interior Art: Terry Brewer
Cover and Book Design: Joy Freeman

AUGUST HOUSE, INC.   PUBLISHERS   LITTLE ROCK

CONTENTS

For Paul and Joshua.
Josh—May your daddy's stories live on forever.

A(KNOWLEDGMENTS

This book would not have been possible without the loving support of my parents, who did what they could for Paul and me. See, Mom, lying does pay off. I wish I could find the right words to express to Nancy, Paul's wife, how much we all appreciate all she did for him. And then there is my wife, Paula, who has to put up with me and my stories. She has done nothing but support and encourage me every step of the way.

Furthermore, I would like to thank Ken Sullivan for starting the West Virginia State Liars Contest and *Goldenseal* for publishing the winning "lies."

Thanks also to the rest of my family (including the in-laws), all my friends, and all Paul's friends, who have amused us, loved us, and inspired many of these tales. Don't worry, I won't name any of you specifically lest your parents discover you, in fact, have been hanging out with "those lying Lepp boys," excepting Donna who, in a momentary lapse of reason, agreed to proofread all this.

—*Bil Lepp*

FOREWORD

"**A** man spends many sleepless nights on the riverbank trying to understand women and many sleepless nights in bed trying to understand carp."

If that doesn't strike you as funny, go on back to Jane Austen. She never wrote a line about carp that I know of, and chances are you are carp-impaired.

If, however, the quotation (from "Carp in the Garden of Eden," pp. 81) tickles you somewhere down deep, then cast *Pride and Prejudice* aside. *The Monster Stick* is the book for you.

In these pages you will find lots more about women and carp (and catfish, trout, and bass, both largemouth and small, walleyes, suckers—even somehow gar, salmon, and one hippo) and more than a little on dogs, trains, and cars, not to mention considerable hunting and more politics than shows on the surface. There is plenty here to keep a thinking man awake nights.

The tales come to us from the gifted West Virginia storytellers Paul and Bil Lepp, proof that lightning—lying, anyway—sometimes does strike twice in the same place, or at least the same family.

The Lepp brothers are about the best natural prevaricators I've ever seen, and I've seen plenty. As the founding impresario of the West Virginia State Liars Contest, I've watched hundreds of yarn spinners take the stage. I've heard some whoppers, beginning with our first grand prize winner back in 1983—Richard Barber's memorable account of a dead mule in a bath-tub—and working on through just about every other animal, dead and alive, as well as false teeth and false lovers, in-laws and outlaws, intemperate weather, moonshining, balky machinery, preachers, politicians, and outhouses.

We hold the Liars Contest at Charleston, in the shadow of the state capitol, each Memorial Day weekend. Top prize, the coveted Golden Shovel, brings out storytellers from every corner of West Virginia, but none better than the Lepps. Paul first showed up in 1986, galvanizing the audience with the first of his Kanawha River fishing sagas. He was back the next year with his New River Gorge story ("There Stands a Bridge," pp. 22), my favorite if I have to pick one. Brother Bil—that's right, one "l"—followed in 1990, and after that their strongest competition usually was each other. It is hard for anyone else to make much headway when a Lepp gets to lying.

The brothers gladly would pass for good old boys, but the truth—dare we mention the word?—is a little more complicated. They come from a respectable preacher's family, and no one was more surprised than the Reverend John Lepp when his sons' particular gift came to widespread public attention. Paul probably falls closer to the down-home stereotype, working over the years as a small town cop, a night desk clerk, and sometimes not at all. "A job's a fine thing, but it cuts into a man's free time something fierce," Paul said, and he valued his leisure.

He came by his trademark fishing tales the honest way, on the riverbank. The Monster Stick is Paul's tool, a nine-foot, surf-casting rod set up with six miles of Stren carp cord and twenty-pound sinkers made special at Weirton Steel. This is major equipment, "the castingest outfit I ever did own," according to Paul. He caught bears, boats, motor homes, and an airborne DC-6 with this rig but mostly some serious catfish and carp. The Stick is compared on the first line of the book to Excalibur, and that's about right.

Paul's little brother is more complex. Bil is better educated, burdened as he is with a West Virginia Wesleyan diploma and a Duke University divinity degree, and to that extent more deliberate and less uninhibited. He never was the fisherman Paul was and admits it. Knowing that the biggest, meanest catfish hit on the rankest bait, Bil uses only the fresh stuff. "When my fear is at its worst, I fish with rosebuds," he says in "I'm Scared of Fish" (pp. 147). It was Bil who brought this book together after an earlier start by Paul.

The boys share deep roots, a loving family, and plenty of long-suffering relatives for story material. The following exchange (from "Lightning Bugged," pp. 97) is attributed to Jackson County cousins:

> "Got 'im."
> "Got who?"
> "I just shot a lightning bug off that walnut tree."
> "Was he flying or just sitting there?"
> "He was sitting."
> "Uh huh, just as I figured. I'll bet he was lit up, too, wasn't he?"

The cousins are a little lit themselves and soon commence shooting fireflies out of the air. But the real shoot-out is the verbal one, just like the West Virginia State Liars Contest. Imagination is the ammunition, and Paul and Bil have more than most.

I speak of the Lepp brothers in the present tense as often as not and don't expect to stop soon, but the fact is we lost Paul more than a year ago. He was the manic genius of the two, a natural who seemed to have to work at it less than his brother. Paul died young after a world of trouble, some no doubt of his own making. I'm pleased to say he had gotten squared up in the last years, back to work and back before his fans, and it was a real shock to lose him at age 36. His death was big news in West Virginia for we don't have enough storytellers to lose the best of them. No place does.

You will find Bil's eulogy at the back of the book. He reminded us at the funeral that God cared enough to send his Son among the fishermen of Galilee. Surely there is room over Jordan for a carp catcher from the banks of the Great Kanawha. Bil is a bona fide Methodist minister, but I'd believe that even if he weren't.

You also will find Bil's documentation at the back. That is useful, especially as you begin to wonder what the origins of each tale may be. I've followed the boys' storytelling for more than a dozen years, and I can't always tell them apart in print. Generally, the fishing stories are Paul's and the dog tales Bil's. Other than that, you had better look it up.

Like all good storytellers, the Lepps ultimately are talking about the human condition—or the West Virginia condition, in any case. We seem a lot funnier in their mouths. They don't shy from our more colorful characteristics, and you will find foibles here we don't always confess to strangers. But it is a loving portrayal, a picture of hardy, hard-headed people most of us would be proud to own up to. We may lack sophistication, but Lord knows we are able and willing. Like two brothers I can think of.

Hillbillies? Fine, as Paul says in "Lightning Bugged."
Call us what you will, but you'll know who to call.

—*Ken Sullivan*

SECTION 1

PAUL

FLYING HIGH

King Arthur had Excalibur, Wyatt Earp had the Peacemaker, and Paul Bunyan had his axe. I, humble, honest, and practical West Virginia boy that I am, I have the Monster Stick. The Monster Stick is my nine-foot, surf-casting rod full of six miles of brand new fifty-pound test Stren carp cord. It's the castingest outfit I ever did own. Casting involves a two-handed side-armed motion and a 360-degree turn by the operator. Once released, the bait rockets out over the water in a graceful arc. I can sit down and drink a beer while waiting for it to land. On a good night, when the wind is just right, I can be into my second can before the sound of the splash comes drifting back to me. If I'm not careful, though, I can hang my line up in the trees on the other side of the river.

Armed with such an extraordinary outfit, I set out on every possible occasion to scour the rivers and lakes of the Mountain State in search of targets worthy of pursuit. Being young and full of energy, and lacking the desire to do much of anything else (like work), I made these jaunts and journeys often. Naturally, a few of these trips were relatively uneventful and sometimes even unproductive, but the

Monster Stick seemed to possess an almost magical ability to conjure up events that, at first, seemed a bit unusual to me. However, as time went on, the unusual began to occur so often that strange events became a sort of trademark of the Monster Stick. I got to the point where I was disappointed if something odd, even amazing, *didn't* happen.

Anyway, I'm going to tell you a story that took place right here in Charleston a few summers back. Now, I've never told the true story before, but seeing how the trial is over, I guess it's safe.

It all began up there at the Marmet Locks on the Kanawha River, right up from Charleston. The night was warm and crisp, a veritable fisherman's dream. There must have been a thousand fishermen up there. They all had their Coleman coolers full and their Coleman lanterns lit. In fact, we fishermen had that riverbank lit up all the way from the Marmet Locks to the 35th Street Bridge.

I was fishing for monster catfish that night and, of course, I had the Monster Stick out. Fishing was a little slow, so I reeled in and put a fresh hunk of rotten liver on my hook, just to kill time. As I was baiting up, I could hear a droning noise coming from above the locks, and I couldn't quite figure out what it was. It wasn't bothering me though, so I went ahead and hooked up and gave one of those patented five-minute casts that the Monster Stick is famous for. Hook, line, and sinker went flying through the air.

And then I saw the plane. It was a DC-6, and it was coming over the locks so low that it was pushing a wake. I knew right away what had gone wrong. That pilot had seen all the fishermen's lights lined up like they were and mistook the river for the runway at the airport. He quickly figured out what he had done, and so he hauled back and shot up into the air. There was an audible, collective sigh of relief from the fishermen as the plane went skyward. As far as anyone could tell, he got back up just fine, but I was not so pleased. The pilot had managed to fly under my arcing cast, and the end of my six miles of brand new carp cord had wrapped a triple clench knot around his tail fin.

If you've never been hooked to the tail of a flying DC-6 before, I'm here to tell you that things start happening mighty fast. The next thing I knew, I was ripped out of my shoes and looking at the pigeons roosting on the 35th Street Bridge, eye to eye. That is to say, my eyes were even with the top beam of that bridge, on which said birds were sitting, and I was coming in quick. There wasn't anything I could do except try and reel myself up over the bridge, so I shut my eyes and reeled. I just made it over. I looked back, and I was so shook up and so happy that I quit reeling. Right away I sunk back down to river level.

As I said, things were happening quickly, and the next thing I knew, the South Side Bridge was zooming up at me like an instant replay. I snapped to it and reeled. I just barely slid over. I was starting to get a little bit worried now.

Just then, the pilot got his bearings straight, and when we came even with the old Sears building, he hung a sharp right for the airport. That whipped me around, and I followed him up the Elk River. For you folks who ain't from around here, I'm here to tell you that there's no fewer than five bridges in the first half-mile of the Elk River.

I began to crank that reel like Bill Dance fishing spinnerbaits at a "Casting for Dollars" contest, and I got reeled up over the Elk River Bridge fine. My momentum carried me over the Virginia Street Bridge. I just barely tipped the Lee Street Bridge, and that somersaulted me over the Washington Street Bridge. That's when my luck ran out. I knew I was going to hit the Spring Street Bridge, and there was nothing I could do about it.

It was about then that my mad caught up with me. I guess I had left all my anger back there on the river-bank somewhere, but now it caught up to me with a vengeance, about forty feet downriver from the Spring Street Bridge. When my anger hit me, it straightened me right out. I was flying through the air like a board. I began to feel like Chuck Yeager, and I started reeling again. I knew I wasn't going to clear the Spring Street Bridge, so I bent my knees a little. When I hit the top beam, I just wrapped my legs around it.

That's when the fisherman in me took over. I reeled in all the slack out of that line and hauled back and set the hook on that plane. When he felt the sting of my #2 Eagle Claw, the fight was on. He took up off the river with a whine and a roar, stripping line so fast I thought the reel might melt. The drag screamed like a cat in an exhaust fan as he began to circle Charleston. While he was stripping the line out, he almost hung me up on the Kanawha Valley Bank building, but I turned him in the nick of time.

Then he came right back at me. I had six miles of brand new fifty-pound Stren carp cord falling all over Charleston. I was reeling it up as fast as I could. He got over me and headed back toward the airport, but I had him now. I could feel him tiring. I was tired, too, and sweating. In fact, I was sweating so hard that cars on the Spring Street Bridge turned their wipers on because they believed it was raining. I got him turned as he was coming around Airport Hill. The line was tight as he went out of sight over the moun-tain and behind the trees. I knew I had him then, so

I started to relax. That's when the line snapped and slung me backwards into the Elk River. All I could do was grab my rod, swim to the bank, and go home.

This was not the first big one that had gotten away from me, and I know that when it's over, it's over. But to my surprise, it wasn't quite over. You see, a friend of mine was working at the airport that night for Eagle Aviation, and it turns out he saw the whole thing. He said what happened was that I was bringing that plane in for a perfect three-point landing, which made me pretty proud because I'd never landed a plane before. I was bringing him in perfectly, and then, at the last minute, that sneaky thing wiggled its tail and hung me up on one of those Air National Guard C-130s. That's when the line broke. The snapping line caused the plane to shoot forward just as it had caused me to fall into the Elk River. That plane went clear off the end of the runway and down into Coonskin Park.

Even that wasn't the end of it, 'cause the next day, I read in the newspaper that that airplane was plumb full of that marijuana stuff from South America, and I just hope my mom's not reading this. I don't care if she knows that I'm hooked on fishing, but I don't want her to think I ever was hooked on pot.

THERE STANDS A BRIDGE

After our brief encounter with drugs, the Monster Stick and I laid low for awhile. I toyed with the idea of having the plane stuffed and mounted, but the cost was prohibitive, and I really couldn't think of a good place to hang it.

I got married instead. Dealing with the fact that I had been played out, lip-landed, and snapped on the ol' stringer by a woman took a bit of time to get used to. I spent a lot less time fishing that fall and winter. It was not until the next spring, and shortly after the birth of my son, that the Monster Stick reared up and drove me to fish again.

I woke up one morning and realized it was the second Saturday in May. There was no special connotation to the day except that it occurred to me that I had not yet been fishing in the new year. I decided that, since it was such a gorgeous day, I was obligated to drive down to the Kanawha River and catch myself some carp. I loaded my gear into the Great Golden Carp Cruiser—the GC for short—kissed my wife and new son goodbye, and headed out.

I drove down to the local 7-Eleven store for supplies. I only had five dollars, so I bought the cheapest six-pack I could find, a can of Vienna sausages for me, and a great big can of Green Giant corn for the carp. I still had a dollar left over, so I bought one of those scratch-off lottery tickets.

I went back out to the car, scratched the ticket, and folks, it was my lucky day. That ticket was worth one thousand dollars! I knew right off there were only two things I could do. One of them was to take that ticket home to my wife and never see a penny of that money again. The other was to cash that ticket, spend all I wanted to, and tell her I won whatever was left over. I cashed that ticket quicker than a Confederate dollar at Appomattox. I bought a full tank of gas for the GC, and I lit out to see "Almost Heaven" with 980 crisp, new, one-dollar bills in my pocket. It was a respectable wad, and I was smiling like a carp in a sewer hole in a rainstorm, until I got to the bridge.

There stands a bridge in Fayette County, West Virginia, that is the longest single-span arch bridge in the whole world. It's the second highest bridge in the country and a spectacular sight. It's called the New River Gorge Bridge, and if you've never been to see it, then you owe yourself a trip. If you go, there's only one thing you need to know, a thing I was about to learn: don't stop in the middle of that bridge for any reason. I'm an experienced man, and I'll tell you why.

I had just started across when I heard this ominous sound that went *thump, thump, thump.* I had a flat tire. I eased on the brakes and coasted to a stop dead in the middle of that seventeen hundred-foot bridge, right there, 876 feet above the good old New River.

A flat's a flat, so I got out and sweated in the hot sun. And you know what? One of these days I'm going to buy a tire iron for the GC because by the time I got those lug nuts off with a pair of channel locks, I was hot, tired, and mad. I guess I was a little too mad because I reached down with both hands and grabbed that spare tire, then turned around and slammed it down onto the pavement.

Well, that tire bounced.

It bounced twenty feet into the air and then came down two feet from the edge of the bridge, which would have been fine except that it was the wrong two feet. I stood looking over the side of the bridge and watched that tire fall 876 feet down to the New River, where it bounced twice and landed upright in three feet of water. I looked 850 feet to my right, to one end of the bridge, and then half a mile down to the bottom of the gorge. Then I looked 850 feet to my left, to that end of the bridge, and then a half-mile down to the gorge. I did some quick ciphering and calculated that it would take anywhere from nine hours to two days to hike down there, get my tire, and bring it back up. That was providing I didn't break any bones.

And then I thought about the Monster Stick.

Now, the Monster Stick is my nine-foot, surf-casting rod full of six miles of brand new fifty-pound Stren carp cord. I could tie a hook to the end of that line, lower away, snag the tire, and reel it up where I stood without even taking a step. Suddenly I began to feel good. I believe that's the same good feeling that old John Brown had right before he put his Harper's Ferry plan into action.

I tied on the hook and lowered away. Everything went just fine for about 830 feet, but then the biggest redbird I ever saw swooped down, mistook the hook for a spider rappelling off the bridge, snapped it up, and flew off into a nearby rhododendron tangle. I thought about my mother and her bird feeders, and I tried to gently coax that bird out of that bush. Then I thought about my state income tax. You know that little box marked the "nongame wildlife fund?" Well,

I'd checked that box every year I'd ever paid taxes, and I thought to myself, "Paul, this is that bird you bought. You're gonna have to do what you have to do!" So I took the slack out of that line and hauled back on the Monster Stick.

That bush fairly erupted into a mushroom cloud of crimson feathers and purple blossoms floating gently down to the river. Out popped my hook, with that bird and a couple of blossoms attached, on a perfect trajectory about a foot above the water and heading straight for my tire.

Lightning struck twice. The water exploded as a four-foot brook trout jumped out of the river and mistook that blob for his Fly-of-the-Month subscription. He paid cash on delivery. He snapped up that blob, dove back into the water, swam sixteen feet upriver, hit his head on a rock, somersaulted through my tire, and landed up on the bank where he just laid there, flopping. I stood 876 feet above him, looking down, wondering what else could possibly happen.

I saw the bushes on the bank rustling and the biggest black bear I ever saw stepped out. He went directly to my fish, nosed it once or twice, and then swallowed it. I began to feel good again. I began to feel good because I knew there was nothing—nothing in the woods, nothing in the water, nothing in the air—that was going to try and eat that bear. I started reeling.

I reeled that bear off the shore and into the water. I reeled that bear's head right through my tire 'til it settled on his shoulders, and then I started reeling up. The Monster Stick was bringing all of it up just fine. I barely had broken a sweat when, rather unexpectedly, I heard a voice. Now, this was no ordinary voice. This was the kind of voice that wakes you up in the middle of the night and tells you, "We've received your tax forms for last year. They are most interesting. See you tomorrow."

The voice said, "Son, what do you think you are doing?"

I said, "Well, I'm trying to get my tire back."

The voice said, "It looks to me like you are fishing."

"No sir," I said.

The man who belonged to that voice stepped 'round beside me and looked over the edge of that bridge. I believe it is fair to say that he was a mite surprised when he saw what was coming up. I was a bit surprised, too, because the man was a ranger. There was nothing I could do but keep right on reeling, so I did. All the fight had gone out of that bear at about five hundred feet, so when I brought him up over the side of the bridge, he just laid there. Not knowing what else to do, I reached for my tire.

"Freeze," said the ranger.

I froze.

The ranger looked at me like I was crazy, then he looked at that bear. He reached into his back pocket and got out a little notebook. He reached in his front pocket and got out a little pencil. He then commenced to writing. He wrote for a long time, pausing every now and again to ask me how tall I was, how much I weighed, where I lived, and the like. Sometimes he just stopped and shook his head. And then, finally, he stopped writing.

"Son," he said, "I don't know how you done this. I don't want to know how you done this. But I do know what you've done, and you're in more trouble than the West Virginia legislature right now." He continued, "Let's see if we understand each other. You see that bear right there? That's a black bear. That's the state animal of the great state of West Virginia, which you have taken illegally, out of season, and without a permit. That's a $500 fine."

Then he said, "You see that fish hanging out of that bear's mouth? That's a brook trout. That's the state fish of the great state of West Virginia, which you have taken from a no-fishing zone by unlawfully obtained bait. That's a $100 fine."

And then he said, "That bait you obtained unlawfully is a cardinal, which is the state bird of the great state of West Virginia. That's a $100 fine. Those flowers hanging out of that bird's beak, they appear to be rhododendron, which is the state flower of the great state of West Virginia, and that's another $100 fine."

He said, "To top it all off, that tire around that bear's neck constitutes litter, which you caused to be tossed into a state scenic river. I hate the litter the most. That's a $150 fine."

He said, "Those fines, in aggregate, shall total $950, payable in cash, right now, immediately, on the spot, or you shall be lawfully confined until such time as payment is made." He stopped for a breath. He looked at my tattered blue jeans and then at the rusty old GC, tottering as it was on three wheels, and he said, "Son, you look like the type that will opt for legal confinement until such a time that payment is made."

I told you he already was looking at me like I was crazy, so when I broke into an ear-to-ear grin, the ranger reached for his gun. But there was no need because I dug down into my pocket and pulled out my lottery wad. I counted out 950 of those 980 crisp, new, one-dollar bills and handed them over. He was even so kind as to take me to a service station owned by his brother-in-law, where they fixed my flat tire for the amazing low price of $28.

As I was in the GC, headed home to South Charleston, I thought back on my day, and I thought that if every fishing trip were going to be that expensive, I certainly couldn't afford to go very often. And then I thought about my wife. Now, I've told you good people this story, and I'm sure you believe me because I'm a reliable man. But my wife, on the other hand, she's the suspicious sort. If I woulda' gone home that night and told her this story, well, I bet she wouldn't have believed it. It was against my grain, but I decided I was going to have to lie to her.

When I walked in the door, she said, "Hi. How did it go?"

All I said was, "Fine. And, oh, by the way," as I reached into my pocket and pulled out those last two crisp, new, one-dollar bills, "Look what I won for you today in the lottery."

THREE WISHES

I sometimes wonder if the manner in which I acquired the Monster Stick has anything to do with the unusual incidents it has spawned. As with most people who take their fishing seriously, I have owned a great many rods and reels through the years. I have ordered them from catalogs, received them as gifts, found a couple, even made a few. The Monster Stick did not come to me by any of these avenues.

There was a fleeting moment in my life when I was single, employed, and living by myself. It was glorious, if not glamorous. It was intense, though short-lived. My castle was a tiny, dilapidated dump, and the price was right. Frequently I was besieged by the inconsiderate attacks of various utility companies that cowardly cut off power to my domain due to slight oversights by my Minister of the Treasury, but hardship builds character in a man's soul. Armed with candles, a five-gallon bucket of water, and a kerosene heater, I refused to bow to their demands. I was monarch of myself, and my kingdom was a happy one. There was no milk and honey, but the beer and peanut butter flowed freely.

In those days, I worked the evening shift and got off at midnight. By the time I got home, changed clothes, and was ready to relax, it usually was nearing one in the morning. This time was not conducive to finding many folks to hang out with, especially on weeknights, so I had to make do. Abe Lincoln went on to be president after reading by candlelight, but it only gave me a headache. I could have driven around looking for something to do, but the Great Golden Carp Cruiser only got four miles to the gallon, going downhill, and most roads in West Virginia only go uphill. Besides, money spent on gas was money not spent on necessities, like peanut butter and fishing gear. The GC was so adamant about not running without fuel that I often thought perhaps it was sympathetic to, if not in cahoots with, the utility companies.

Ah, but by the merest of coincidences, my dwelling was within walking distance of my secret fishing hole. With the basic expenditures of a fishing license, canned corn, and replacement hooks, line, and sinkers, I was provided with an ever flowing source of entertainment. I was young and healthy, and like the mailman, I could not be prevented from setting forth by the elements. As long as the water was wet, the fish were there. And as long as the fish were there, well, I felt obliged to be there too.

Therefore, on one winter's night when the softer types were snug beneath their blankets or huddled in front of their fireplaces, I ventured out to fish, despite the fact that the thermometer outside my kitchen window registered only six degrees. I dressed heavily and selected a vintage can of corn, one sure to attract a semi-arctic carp. I settled on a can of military surplus C-ration corn because I had heard that 1952, after the rains, was an excellent year for carpcorn. I knew I would need every possible advantage to catch anything that night. Fortunately, I was highly impressed with my angling ability and sallied forth with good confidence.

My confidence faded a mite when I got down to the river. The first thing I noticed was that six degrees was a whole lot colder on the riverbank than it was in my moderately kerosene-heated house. Although the river was not frozen, large chunks of ice drifted by in the dark like inland icebergs in search of freshwater Titanics. Falling snow created a gentle hiss as it landed on the water like the sound of fuzz on a stereo's needle. Trees along the bank cracked and groaned in the frigid air. This was no Saturday afternoon T.V. fishing show looking for tarpon in the Florida Keys. This was True Grit West Virginia carp fishing, and I was True Grit!

I cut the corn open and baited up. My first cast landed on a passing piece of ice. I had to reel in, and when I did, I found that all the corn had fallen off. I reached into the can to get some more only to discover that the contents already had frozen. It took several minutes to thaw a few pieces off with my Bic. I finally rebaited, and my next cast was perfect. I set the rod down on a snowdrift and turned my mind to other matters. My beers were freezing.

Beer slurpies don't do too much for me. One partially frozen beer on a hot summer's day can be refreshing, but the same cold beer on a winter's night is unacceptable. Harsh climates call for desperate measures. I unbuttoned my jacket and shirts and placed a beer under each armpit. I loosened my belt and slid the remaining cans into the waistband of my underwear, against my warm skin. It was not a pleasant feeling, and it made me somewhat awkward, but the beer was saved.

The fishing, like the weather, was not hot. My rod lay still and silent upon the snowdrift. I stamped my feet in a very unfisherman-like fashion to keep my toes from freezing, the fallen snow muffling my foot-beats. Through the darkness came the whispers of the black river as it ferried its load of broken ice west-ward. I felt a bond between the river and myself as together we braved the night. An almost enchanted feeling crept over me, as though a spell had been cast.

I had to pee—the spell was broken. Hey, it happens when you have a couple of beers in you and two more cold ones pressing against your bladder under your belt. I blew on my fingers to loosen them up and stumbled to the nearest tree. Loaded down with my cargo of cans, the trip was not an easy journey. As I was going about my business, I glanced over at my rod just in time to see it receive a jolting strike, spring four feet into the air, and shoot out toward the water!

I spun around, causing a most unpleasant chill fac-tor, and I charged forward, tripping over beer cans as they issued from my pantlegs. I snatched the rod just before it entered the frigid river. I dug my heels into the snow, heaved back, and set the hook. Despite the temperature, that fish took off like a rocket on the Fourth of July. His initial run was so strong that it heated my drag until the whole reel glowed like a potbellied stove. Snow fell against the reel and van-ished in tiny puffs of steam that encircled my head, adding to the mystical effects of the night.

The struggle continued until it became more than a challenge; it became a quest, an odyssey. My line thumped as the unseen river giant hugged the bot-tom, digging his nose into the mud and begrudging-ly yielding ground. I fought to bring him up and began to sweat from the effort, icicles forming off my ears and nose. My arms grew numb and the blood pounded in my brain as the battle raged.

He at last came into the shallows. I began to catch

glimpses of his monstrous fins as he doggedly rolled and struggled, roiling the water and sucking down massive whirlpools with his tail. At last he was beached, and I beheld him fully. He lay gasping in several inches of water, and I sank to my knees to look at him. I had never seen such a carp in all my life. His golden scales were as big as trash can lids, and he was at least eight feet long. I guessed he weighed more than a hundred pounds. Most unusual of all were his eyes. They were as big as bowling balls and sky blue! He was staring at me, eye to eye.

"Yo," he said. Just like that. "Yo," in a deep, rasping voice.

"What?" I said, rather suspiciously.

"Let me go, and I'll give you two wishes."

Well, I was planning to let him go anyway, but it occurred to me that there just might be something to this proposal. I figured it was worth a try, considering this was a talking carp.

"All right," I said, "but you are supposed to give me three wishes."

"Who says?" the carp wanted to know.

"I do. It's always been that way. Nobody only gives two wishes. It has to be three, that's the rules. The Rules, you know."

He did not know that, or so he said, but he was in no position to bargain, and so he agreed. Next, he told me to let him go and use the wishes as I wanted. I wasn't about to fall for that one, especially since he'd already tried to rip me off one wish.

"I think I'll just take them right now," I told him, "while I've still got you on the line, so to speak. What do I have to do?"

"You have to hurry, that's what. I don't know if I'll freeze or suffocate first, but one or the other is bound to happen soon, and if I go belly up, you get nothin'!"

Now, everyone wants three wishes, but when the time comes to take them, very few folks have them written down so they can wish them one, two, three. I didn't. I do now, of course—I keep a list in my wallet in case it ever happens again—but right then I did not have a list. I pondered. The fish fidgeted.

"O.K.," I said, "Let's try an easy one. I'm cold, make me warm."

There was a flash of light, a cloud of smoke, and *presto!* I was standing waist-deep in a barrel of warm water.

"That's not what I meant," I said. "This is too hot, and I'll freeze when I get out. I wish you hadn't done that."

Another flash, another cloud, and the water was gone. I stood on the bank once more, dry as a bone. "There," said the carp, "That's two. Make the third one and let me go."

I wanted to argue, but the old boy was obviously suffering, and he had done exactly as I had asked. I looked around for an idea and happened to see my cheap little fishing pole lying in the snow. The plastic had melted off its handle during the heated fight, and the reel was deformed, too.

"Listen," I said, carefully choosing my words. "No tricks. Don't start until I tell you to. I want a new rod and reel, but not an ordinary one. I want one like no other rod and reel that's ever been. It has to be strong enough to catch anything and never fail me. It needs to be real cool and look good to boot. That's what I wish for. Now, please do it."

The flash. The cloud. The Monster Stick. The outfit that every fisherman wants but only I have. Unless, of course, someone else lands the magic carp. He's still out there. I turned him loose, as promised, and he sank into the murky depths of the Kanawha, waiting for another day, another angler.

As for me, well, I took the Monster Stick and went home. I figured I'd had enough luck for one night. Little did I know right then, but I'd had about as much luck as a man ever could. There just ain't another pole like the Monster Stick. Never was, never will be. That's just as well, I suppose. No offense, but I just don't think most folks are cut out to wield one. It's a sort of sword-in-the-stone thing. The Monster Stick is mine.

Unnatural Disaster

I've always believed it takes three things to get by in the world today: life, liberty, and a secret fishing hole. As for life, you can see plainly I'm alive and kicking as I stand here before you today. As for liberty, I'm just as free as my wife will let me be. And I've got a dandy secret fishing hole. Being secret and all, there's not a whole lot I can tell you about it, other than that it's located on the banks of the scenic Kanawha River somewhere in the general vicinity of South Charleston. It's quiet, peaceful, and secluded. It'd probably make a really good swimming hole too, if you could get the fish to move out of your way long enough to get in the water.

I was down there the other day, relaxing in a lawn chair. I had my feet up on the cooler, I had the Monster Stick in my hand, and I was making small talk with a bucket of nightcrawlers. By and by, a big old coal boat came plowing up the river behind five barges of coal. As she drew near, I saw that she was a big oil company's boat called *City of Charleston*. If you've never seen that boat, she's a fine one: four decks and a big shiny wheelhouse. As she got up to me, I waved at her like I always do a passing riverboat. Imagine my surprise when her engines backed down and she slid to a stop right there.

Framed in the doorway stood the captain, white shirt, gold braids, and all. He came down to me, and his voice was real bashful-like. He requested permission to come ashore. I guess I'm a little old-fashioned, but I've always ranked riverboat captains right up there with God, train engineers, and policemen. So I told him I'd be right honored if he'd come down.

He climbed over and stood beside me, and folks, he was a sorry sight. He looked like he didn't have a friend in the world and was about to cry. He stuck out his hand to introduce himself, and it was then I realized why he looked so glum. You see, the man standing in front of me, on the banks of the Kanawha River, at my very own secret fishing hole, was none other than the captain of the late great Valdez, the ship that let loose enough oil in Prince William's Sound to keep Alaska from squeaking until the twenty-fifth century.

He looked so low that I offered him a beer. He took that beer and drank it down in one swallow. And he said it tasted good. He said it was the first one he'd had since the wreck. I hate to see a grown man thirsty, so I offered him another one. He took that one and about four more, and by the time he'd finished the sixth one, he was feeling a considerable lot better. He was feeling so good that I felt brave enough to ask him the question I was dying to ask: "Just exactly what happened up there in Alaska?"

He said it happened like this. Everything was going fine on the bridge of the Valdez that day. In fact, it was going so smoothly that when a big school of salmon swam by, he figured there wouldn't be any harm in turning the bridge over to his new third mate while he ran down to take a few casts. That's exactly what he did. On the first cast, he hooked a fine salmon, but as he was reeling it in, the salmon was swallowed by a migrating killer whale. Little did the captain know, but his new mate up on the bridge was an ex-deep-sea fishing boat captain out of Tampa, Florida. When the mate saw the whale, he assumed that was what they were fishing for, and he turned the whole ship to follow. The rest is history. Before anything could be done, the boat was aground and ten million gallons of oil were afloat. That big oil company stripped the captain of his ship and stuck him down on the Kanawha River assuming, I suppose, that he'd end up like everyone else in West Virginia and get laid off.

Looking at it in that light, the whole thing made a lot more sense, at least to me, because that sort of thing happens to me all the time. I told the captain how I felt, and he was so tickled that he offered to take me for a ride on his boat. I've always wanted to fish the main channel of the Kanawha from a big boat. When the *City of Charleston* set sail again, I was signed on as a bonafide charter fisherman and strapped into a makeshift fighting chair at the stern of that boat. With the Monster Stick in hand, I began trolling for giant Kanawha River catfish.

I didn't expect to have any luck fishing over those big twin diesel engines and all, but I was wrong. We had just cleared the Patrick Street Bridge when the fish hit, and he hit with such power and fury that the boat immediately started to lose steam. The captain didn't know what was happening, so he hit full steam ahead. That boat began to buck and shake like a rodeo bronco. Everything that was not lashed down began to dance off the decks and out into the water like spiders off a hot griddle.

The captain looked out the back wheelhouse door and saw what was going on. His eyes got as big around as saucers. He flung open the door and hollered, "Boy, cut that line!"

Folks, right then I realized that, sad but true, the things they said about that captain were right. He did have a drinking problem. If he thought I was going to cut loose a catfish that could out-tow a towboat, well, he must have been drunk! I hollered back up, "I can't hear you!"

He dashed back into the wheelhouse and came back with a big butcher knife. He began to make slashing motions in the air and shouted, "Son! I said cut that line!"

"I can't hear you!"

He held the knife to his throat and said, "Boy, if you don't cut that line, I'll come down there and cut your throat!"

I hollered back up, "I can't hear you, but don't kill yourself over it! Somebody's got to steer this thing!"

The engines moaned, the turbines whined, and the props below me were kicking up the Kanawha like a muddy Niagara Falls. Just downstream that fish came up, his giant dorsal fin slicing through the river like a freshwater Jaws and his great forked tail thrashing and frothing that water, throwing the riverboat's wake right back at us 'til we knew something was gonna give.

Well, you folks know enough about me that there's not a soul out there who thinks for a minute that it was going to be me and the Monster Stick that gave way. As it turns out, it wasn't going to be that Kanawha catfish either. He was raised on PCBs, dioxins, and other such vitamins and minerals, and he was fit to fight. The fish dove. When he came back up, he broke clear free of the water and then splashed back down with such a force that it sent a forty-foot tidal wave back upstream toward us. I just had time to cut myself free from the fighting chair when the water hit. Sadly, it sent the *City of Charleston* to the bottom of the Kanawha.

The captain, in time-honored tradition, went down with ship. I immediately realized that he was a lot better off than I was because the boat only went down in twenty feet of water, leaving two decks and the wheelhouse high and dry. I, on the other hand, was in the river with a catfish that had just sunk a towboat and was likely to have worked up a powerful appetite. I thought about that possibility and came to the conclusion that any fish that was that sporting, well, the only sportsmanlike thing for me to do was cut him loose and give someone else a chance to catch him later. I reached down and cut the line. After that, I swam back to check on the captain.

Needless to say, he was a wreck. You see, when the boat went down, all five barges turned turtle and dumped ten thousand tons of West "By God" Virginia coal on the bottom of the Kanawha River, creating the worst bituminous spill in the history of river navigation. For the second time in two months, the Coast Guard showed up and hauled him away.

I grabbed my empty cooler out of the wheelhouse, took the Monster Stick, and headed for home. Later I got to thinking about it, and I think this time the captain is going to come out all right because, in this particular spill, not one sea lion, sea otter, sea gull, seal, nor salmon was killed. The harshest environmental impact I can see is the slight possibility that a few slow-witted and sluggish carp might have been squished to the bottom of the Kanawha River, which is no big deal. In fact, when you think about it, five barges' worth of coal is probably the cleanest thing that's been dumped into the Kanawha River in the last fifty years!

Which brings up the point of the whole story: I think Senator Jay Rockefeller needs to get on the phone to somebody up there in Alaska. Obviously those people use a lot of fuel trying to stay warm during those long, cold winters. Now, coal makes a mighty fine heating fuel. I bet you the Monster Stick that you couldn't find a single soul up there who wouldn't rather have ten thousand tons of West Virgina coal on the bottom of their ocean than ten million gallons of oil on top.

Just the same, Jay, if you do strike a deal with them, you tell those folks we can send them all the coal they want, but if it's all the same to them, we'll send it by train.

WEATHER OR NOT

In the grand old tradition of my beloved state, I've been known to practice unemployment from time to time. At one point, I had practiced so long and so hard and gotten so good at not having a job that I decided I didn't need to practice anymore. The next thing I knew, I had a full-time job. I'm not complaining. A job's a fine thing, but it cuts into a man's free time something fierce, much the same way being married does.

You see, there was a time when I could go fishing whenever I wanted to. Nowadays, between my job and my family, fishing trips are scarce. That's why, when I found myself this very morning at the tiny town of Centralia, West Virginia, at the headwaters of the Sutton Lake, in a blinding rainstorm, I decided I was going to fish no matter what. I had come through a lot just to get there, and I wasn't going to give up just because of a little weather. I had taken the day off work, and because my car, the Great Golden Carp Cruiser, had broken down, I had been forced to ask my wife if I could use her VW Rabbit. It was only after a lot of tears and threats—my tears and her threats—that I had talked my wife into letting me use her car. She agreed I could take her car, but only after I had filed a AAA-approved trip plan. She allowed me three hundred miles on the odometer, which is round trip from South Charleston to Centralia, and twelve hours (six to drive, six to fish). That way, she said, she'd know I went where I said I was going. She also made me swear I'd be home on time. She made me swear, all right.

So, like I said, rain or no rain, after all that, I was going to fish. Besides, I had a plan. I pulled that Volkswagen right down to the water's edge and put on the parking brake. Next, I reached out the window and untied the Monster Stick from the luggage rack (nine feet of fishing machine is too much for the inside of a compact car). I reached into the back, opened the bait bucket, and pulled out one of those giant ten-pound, ten dollar crawdads that I had bought from the seafood shop at the Big Bear in Charleston.

I hooked that thing up, rolled down the window, stuck the Monster Stick out, and gave a five-minute cast down the lake. I jumped out of the car and propped the Monster Stick in the space between the grill and the bumper on that Rabbit. Congratulating myself on being so smart, I came back around, got in the car, rolled up the window, turned on the windshield wipers, and sat back as warm and dry as a crumb in a toaster oven.

The West Virginia Mountaineers were on the radio that day taking on the Pitt Panthers. I reached into the back and extracted a cold drink from the cooler, being extra sure I reached into the correct container. Those giant crawdads were in the other cooler and seemed none too happy about their impending fate. They were watchful little beasts, and I knew they would retaliate if I allowed them the chance.

The football game was going well for us, and I was

really starting to enjoy myself. I suppose that should have tipped me off. The second half had just begun. Major Harris, West Virginia's quarterback at the time, dropped back to pass. Pitt blitzed; Harris scrambled. He looked deep downfield, pumped once, twice...suddenly there was a tremendous hit! Well, actually there were two hits. The Maj took one, fumbled, and Pitt took it in for a touchdown. The second hit was the one that concerned me most, though. It came on the Monster Stick.

I flung open the door to go and set the hook. I never made it to the Monster Stick. As soon as I opened the door, I realized that what they say about Volkswagens is all too true: they float.

You see, that fish had hit so hard that he pulled the car right down the muddy bank and onto the water of Sutton Lake. The Monster Stick was bent double, and the car was picking up speed at an alarming rate. I did the only thing I could think of. I fastened my seat belt, turned the wipers on high, and reached into the back for another drink. The Great Crawdad Rebellion began. I had lifted the wrong lid by mistake, and instead of me grabbing a can, five extremely agitated crustaceans grabbed me.

By now, we were a mile down the lake, passing the campgrounds, still gaining speed, and throwing a rooster tail seventy-five yards long. With my free hand, I desperately tried to steer for shore, but that car always had had a habit of hydroplaning, and in one hundred feet of water, traction was scarce. I finally managed to get my other hand free of the bait bucket, and I looked down to take a quick inventory of my fingers. As far as I could tell, they all were there. When I looked up, I was not pleased.

Looming up at me, out of the spray, was the Sutton Dam. Straight ahead the fish swam, never an inch to the left or the right. On and on I went toward the dam 'til a crash was coming for sure. At the last second, the fish dove down deep. The front end of the Rabbit went down; the rear end came up; and the Monster Stick, the Rabbit, and I went airborne, right over the face of the Sutton Dam. I knew I was a dead man. If the wreck didn't kill me, my wife would. I closed my eyes and held on.

Suddenly, the line came tight. The wheels hit the dam, I hit the brakes, the tires bit into the face of the dam, and we skidded to a stop twenty feet above the rocks of the spillway. When I opened my eyes, I discovered that I was eyeball to eyeball with the great-granddaddy of all catfish. He had dove down hoping to escape through the drain hole, but he was so big that he had hung up in that eighteen-foot hole like a cork in a jug. He had pushed the grate right out of that drain and had it jammed in his mouth. He was grinning like a TV preacher with all the phone lines lit up.

I decided we were a little too close for comfort, so I jammed the Rabbit into reverse and drove right back up to the top of the dam. Things were no better up there. You see, the rain was still raining, but the drain wasn't draining. The water was rising, and the pressure was building. The dam began to shake until I just knew something fierce was about to happen. Suddenly, with a tremendous *pop!* that catfish shot out of that hole like an MX missile, headed down the Elk River and straight for Charleston.

It was an interesting sight to see a thirty-foot rocket catfish going downstream that fast—but then the line tightened and the Rabbit, Monster Stick, and I were jerked off the face of the Sutton Dam, down into the dark, deep, cold water, unceremoniously drawn through the drain hole, and jerked right on down the

Elk River, still hooked solid to that nuclear catfish.

The force that had fired that fish from the dam was so powerful that we never touched down on the water once we popped out the other side of the dam. We began to pass Elk River towns like telephone poles on the interstate. We went through Sutton, Gassaway, Frametown, Strange Creek, Duck, Ivydale, Clay, Procious, Queen Shoals, Clendenin, Elkview, and Big Chimney quicker than it takes to tell.

I don't know anything about physics or Albert Einstein and all his relatives, but I do know the ballgame was in the third quarter and the Panthers were up 30-10 when we left Sutton, but by the time we hit Charleston, it was the second quarter again, and the 'Eers still had a chance. It was a quick trip.

When we got back to Charleston, that fish had about a half-mile lead on me as he hung a sharp right for New Orleans via the Kanawha, Ohio, and Mississippi rivers. He cut such a sharp turn that my line came up against a concrete abutment on the I-64 bridge. At nearly 186 thousand miles per second, it was too much even for my fifty-pound Stren carp cord, and the line broke.

Without that catfish to pull us around the corner, the Rabbit, the Monster Stick, and I shot straight across the Kanawha River, up the bank and down Oakwood Road plumb to Red House before we coasted to a stop. Folks, I was never so glad to lose a fish in all my life.

And then I looked at the odometer. As usual, I was in trouble again. It seems that the trip down the Elk River had failed to log any return mileage. To a used car salesman, well, that would have been wonderful. To a man who had to account for his whereabouts to a suspicious wife, it was a disaster. You will recall, of course, the written trip plan. Taxing my brain with my meager mathematical skills, I discovered I was back in town eight hours and 150 miles too soon.

Now, the Charleston/South Charleston area offers many scenic sights, as either city's Chamber of Commerce will be happy to tell you. I will pass on another fact that they might neglect. In eight hours of laps, at twenty miles an hour, you will see those sights more times than you might care to. I certainly did that day. It was, however, one of the few times, if not the only time, the Monster Stick and I were back from a fishing trip exactly on time and darn happy for it!

SECTION 2

BIL

Buck Ain't No Ordinary Dog

I have a dog, and my dog's name is Buck. Buck ain't no ordinary dog. What you have to understand about Buck is that his mama was a German shepherd, but his daddy was a prolific and extremely determined basset hound; and while he inherited his mother's good looks, he got his daddy's legs in the bargain. Buck stands about half a dog high, and he's about a dog and a half long. He looks like a German shepherd that swallowed a Ford Fairlane.

While Buck ain't much to look at, in his own way he's a canine idiot savant. I could tell right from the start that dog was bound to be one of the greatest hunting dogs ever to follow a trail. You see, what he lacks in looks, he makes up for in nasal prowess. That dog has a nose to rival Toucan Sam. Buck can smell a skeleton in a closet four years old. (Coincidentally, he's not allowed in the White House.) I can let that dog smell the eggs we have at breakfast, and he'll run out to the henhouse and bring me the chicken that laid them. One time I let Buck smell one of those spicy chicken wings, and half an hour later, he was back in the living room with a bottle of Tabasco and a buffalo.

I always hoped Buck would grow up to be a hunting dog. In preparation we'd stay up every night watching those hunting tapes on the VCR, then we'd read *Field & Stream* to each other until we fell asleep. The only thing keeping Buck from being the greatest hunting dog that ever lived was the fact that he was just a touch gun-shy. So last April, when we were thick in the middle of that cold spell, I decided to cure Buck of his gun-shyness, and here's what I done.

I went out in the backyard and drew up a target on an old piece of cardboard. I laid that target on the compost pile down in the field. Buck was inside, sound asleep in front of the fire. He had a smile on his snout, and I could tell he was dreaming about tracking game or beautiful dogs on short little legs. I went inside, woke Buck up, took a rope and tied it between his collar and my belt loop, and we went outside. I got my trusty .30-30 rifle; I pulled out one bullet and held it down for Buck to look over. He eyed it up, licked it, and took a couple of strong sniffs. When he gave me a confident nod, I loaded the shell, took aim, and BLAMO! I fired.

As usual, I had neglected to consider the full ramifications of my actions. No sooner was that bullet out of the barrel of my gun then Buck was in hot pursuit. Now, the best I can figure, Buck thought he was supposed to track that bullet. He went flying through midair after that bullet. And when he got to the end of that rope tied from his collar to my belt loop, it jerked taut and pulled me right out of my boots, through the hole the bullet had punched in the target, and then headfirst through the compost pile. I don't know if you folks know what it's like to be dragged headfirst through a pie of dung, but—oh, wait, of course you folks know what it's like, we've just come through an election year.

Buck tracked that bullet into the woods, and every time it glanced off a tree or ricocheted off a rock, he was there with me in tow. He tracked that bullet clear to the railroad tracks—that fine and famed run of Weirton's world-famous steel fashioned into CS&X railroad tracks running clear from Cowen to Grafton via Burnsville, Buckhannon, Carrolton, and Philippi. At the railroad tracks, a 168-car CS&X monster train loaded with 19,364 tons of pure West Virginia bituminous coal was passing by, and that bullet slammed into the side of one of those cars.

Well, the Buck stopped there. I, however, passed the Buck and crashed into the side of that train. When I went flying by Buck, that rope tied from his collar to my belt loop jerked taut one more time and pulled my jeans right off me. When I hit that train, I was screaming—partly out of fear, but mostly because it was twelve degrees, and suddenly I wasn't wearing anything but my boxer shorts. Because I was screaming, my tongue was the first part of my body to hit that train. When my tongue hit that cold metal, it froze fast. Folks, I was stuck to that train worse than scandal to a politician.

I was able to run alongside that train for a bit, but before long I tripped. When I tripped, I rotated on my tongue and began flapping in the wind, parallel to that train. I could see Buck out of the corner of my eye, keeping pace with the train. My mouth was wide open; and the wind was blowing right in, forcing drool to run out over my cheek, cascade over my shoulder, roll down my arm, and spray out behind me. Before I knew what was happening, there was a fifty-foot wing of frozen drool sticking out perpendicular from the right side of that train.

That train probably was going sixty miles per hour, and the wind was catching under that wing pretty good. I looked down and noticed that the wheels on the right side of that train were starting to lift off the tracks ever so easy. When we crested the hill and started down, we picked up speed. All I can figure is that the speed, drag, lift, and all that aeronautical mumbo-jumbo was just right 'cause all five engines, the 168 coal cars, the caboose, me, my tongue, and the fifty-foot wing of frozen drool suddenly were airborne. If anybody had been with me, they'd have surely called us the Wrong Brothers.

Having never flown before, I figured to see what I could do. I took that train through a couple of loopty-loop's, did a steep climb, tried a couple of inverted flat rolls; and then I wrote my wife's name using the exhaust from those engines, just like one of them daredevil pilots on TV. After that, I started thinking about how I didn't even have a pilot's license—or even an engineer's license for that matter—and since I didn't want to get busted by the FAA or the CS&X police, I made ready to set that train back down. I reconnoitered the tracks beneath me, straightened the train out, and took her in.

Buck was running along the tracks below, keeping his eyes right on me. I was a little anxious about landing that train; after all, I had only my tongue to steer with, the train had only one wing, and the one wing it did have was iced over. I just kept repeating to myself, "I think I can, I think I can," and I laid that train down. The landing was a little bumpy, but I felt pretty proud about the whole affair. But that's when the real trouble started. Y'all know how the Good Book says "Pride cometh before the fall"? Well, I was headed right for the fall.

My tongue was still frozen solid to the side of that

train, and I looked up just in time to see the front end entering a tunnel. Now, I don't know what you know about train tunnels, but they're built just wide enough for the train and nothing else. I was sticking out just far enough from the train so that when the car I was frozen to rolled in, my head collided directly with the rock face of the mountain just to the right of that tunnel. The ice wing shattered, and I came to a sudden and violent stop. Buck skidded to a halt beneath me.

My tongue, however, was still frozen solid to that train, and that train kept right on going. As my tongue was pulled further and further from my mouth, I sensed the train was starting to slow, ever so little, under the strain. I knew one of two things was bound to happen: either that train was going to stop, or my tongue was going to be ripped from my mouth. I sighed and said, "Thomethin' hath got to gib."

Just then there was a snap, the train sped on, and my tongue came barreling out of that tunnel hellbent for fury. By this time, my tongue was stretched about forty feet, and it snapped by me like a giant rubber band, shooting me straight into the sky. Before long, gravity caught up to me, and I started to plummet, trailing my tongue behind me. I dropped right between a set of power lines. As I fell, my tongue wrapped a perfect clove hitch around those power lines, and I was left suspended ten feet from the ground. I figured I was stuck 'til someone happened along or my tongue shrank. Either way, I figured I had more hang time on my hands than Michael Jordan. To top it off, a little ol' jaybird came and lit on my head.

I was looking around mindlessly when I noticed a black bear working himself out of his cave. He was lean and hungry from a long winter's hibernation, and I could tell he was looking for something to eat. When he looked up and saw me hanging there in my boxer shorts, with that jaybird on my head, why he just smiled. He must have thought we were some sort of X-rated piñata sent straight from Heaven.

That bear reached into the hollow of a tree and pulled out an aluminum ladder and metal softball bat. He set that ladder just underneath me and started up. He steadied himself on the top step of that ladder (the one that says, clear as day, "Do not stand here, you might lose your balance.") and took a few practice swings with that bat. He was just about to deliver the deathblow when Buck, still tirelessly tracking me, came bounding out of the underbrush (of course, on his short legs it's more like overbrush). He showed up in the nick of time.

Buck quickly assessed the situation, bound up that ladder, and bit that bear on the butt. The bear dropped the bat and lost his balance. He rocked back and forth on that ladder, and just as he was about to fall, he grabbed hold of my ankles. Now when that bear grabbed my ankles while standing on that aluminum ladder, with Buck biting his butt, and my tongue hitched to those power lines, well that completed a seventy thousand volt circuit none of us had anticipated. The current flowed right down my tongue; through the jaybird, me, the bear, and Buck; and then hit the ladder. The resulting explosion blew the feathers off the bird, the fur off the bear, and all the hair off Buck. And then it blew us all straight up into the night sky. So there we were—my forty-foot tongue, the jaybird, me as naked as that jaybird, the buck-naked bear, and the bare-naked Buck—all streaking through the sky like a comet.

Well, eventually everything got back to normal. My

tongue shrank, the bird got its feathers back, the bear got its fur back, and Buck got his hair back. If I learned anything from this whole affair—and it seems like the sort of thing I should have learned something from—I'd guess I'd have to say that sometimes it is best to just let sleeping dogs lie.

BUCK VERSUS THE GOVERNMENT

It was the spring after I had graduated from my master's program, and I had been looking for a job ever since. To that end, I decided to go down to the employment office and take one of those career aptitude tests. When I was done with the test, the career counselor called me into his office and said that my test was the strangest he'd ever graded. He said that, according to the results, I was best suited to pursue a career as either a monster truck driver—you know, as in MONSTER MONSTER MONSTER!!!—or as a politician—you know, as in MONSTER MONSTER MONSTER!!!

I weighed the pros and cons of each of those choices and decided that life on the truck and tractor pull circuit certainly had some pros. And I knew in my heart that, if I went into politics, I would be dealing exclusively with cons. I signed the papers and began my new, exciting, and rewarding career as a truck and tractor competitor. Unfortunately, I wasn't very good. Before long, I was in a slump and falling fast.

Now, those of you who know me know about Buck, my extraordinary hunting dog whose mother was a

German shepherd and whose daddy was a prolific and extremely determined basset hound. Ol' Buck was just about to celebrate his second birthday—his fourteenth in people years—and so now I had a dog who was going through his terrible twos and adolescence simultaneously. To complicate matters, Buck is smarter than most people and stronger than four CS&X engines pulling in unison.

In the past eighteen months, he'd broken more ropes, steel cable, and chains than Congress had promises. One evening I tied him to the back of my shed, and in the morning all I had was a loose dog and a lean-to. So one night, after a particularly grueling truck and tractor pull, I was so fed up with Buck's antics and my career that I got the biggest chain I could find and bolted Buck to the frame of my monster truck. I jerked the chain and said, "There, break out of that." I went inside and had the first good night's sleep I'd had in a long time.

Well, I'd like to establish a little credibility with you folks, and you know as well as I do that I'd be lying if I told you that, when I checked on Buck in the morning he'd broken free of that getup. No sir, when I found him, he was latched to the frame of that truck just as surely as he had been the night before. But I will tell you that he had managed to pull my truck forty feet into the woods and would have kept right on going if he hadn't treed the squirrel he was chasing. I looked at him, chained to my truck and asleep in the woods, then I looked at the glacier-like path he had carved through the trees. I was wondering how far through the woods *I* could pull a pick-up truck with a full load of firewood in the back and with the emergency brake on, when suddenly I had an idea, a stroke of genius really. Wouldn't Buck make a big showing at the next tractor pull if he pulled my truck across the stadium?

Right then I started Buck on a strict training regimen. I slowly weaned him off water and started giving him distilled diesel fuel instead. For meals he ate raw meat, chunks of coal, and fresh ramps. Buddy, if that didn't give him the gas he needed! I threw away all the newspapers spread on the floor of Buck's doghouse and replaced them with muscle and hot rod magazines. At night I just tied him to heavy objects—fallen trees, boulders, the tank in front of the armory—and let him go. He was getting stronger every day. Neighbors hired him to pull out stumps, and stranded motorists called to have him get their cars out of the mud.

While Buck was training, I worked on his pulling rig. I got some of that cord the riverboats use to tie up their barges and spun that into a harness. I used depleted uranium for the buckles. I took the coupling device off of an old railroad car, cleaned it up really good, and welded it to the harness. In that rig, Buck could have pulled the New River Gorge to the top of Spruce Knob. Heck, if I'd have hooked that harness to the tip of the eastern panhandle and gotten Buck running west, why, he'd have flipped the whole state of West Virginia onto Ohio like a buckwheat flapjack.

Needless to say, we took the world of truck and tractor pulls by surprise. Buck won the local, state, and regional championships without breaking a sweat. After the regionals, he looked up at me and said, "I am Tiger Woods." Of course, to everyone else it just sounded like "woof, woof, woof."

The national champion was a guy representing the federal government. It seems the president loves a good tractor pull, and he had commissioned 144 agents from 117 federal agencies to build the world's greatest pulling machine. They had picked up an old train locomotive at a surplus store, jacked it up on six-foot steel wheels, and outfitted it with one of those new five thousand horsepower Caterpillar train engines. They got the boys down at NASA to convert it so that it ran on a lethal mixture of diesel fuel and liquid oxygen. It was a hauling machine and could pull a 168-car CS&X monster train loaded with 19,364 tons of pure West Virginia bituminous coal, along Weirton's world-famous steel fashioned into CS&X railroad tracks clear from Cowen to Grafton via Burnsville, Buckhannon, Carrolton, and Philippi in less time than it takes me to tell you about it.

Now, the rules to the contest were simple. We met on an old stretch of railroad tracks just east of French Creek. The champ backed his locomotive down the tracks, and the judges coupled that engine to Buck's rig. Five yards either way down the tracks a railroad tie was painted hunter's orange. Whichever contestant crossed his tie first won.

The starter gun sounded, and that engine came to life with a bang. Smoke and flame bellowed out of its stacks like Union Carbide in its heyday. The engineer went full throttle and let the brake completely off. Those big steel wheels spun like a drag car's. The whole engine oozed kinetic energy, but Buck leaned forward in his harness, and that engine didn't move. They stayed like that for the rest of the day and into the night. It was a classic John Henry situation, man versus machine, only in this case it was a dog. They stayed frozen like that for days: the rhododendrons bloomed, the mighty Buckhannon River surged and waned on its eternal course, but try as it might, even with its 144 agents from 117 federal agencies and five thousand horsepower engine, that locomotive couldn't make Buck budge.

You see, in situations such as these, Buck's genetics—

being half basset hound—really pays off in spades. Even in the hills of West Virginia, on his short, little legs, Buck's center of gravity is somewhere below sea level. I could tell he was ready to hold out like a right-wing, gun-totin', communist-hatin', conspiracy-theory-hatchin', comet-lovin', Texas separatist militia man, and there was no way 144 agents from 117 federal agencies were about to take him down!!

The match began to look like a draw until one day, ever so easy, Buck began to raise his front paw and point. A hush fell over the crowd as we saw a squirrel mindlessly wandering down the tracks toward him. When the squirrel was within range, Buck sprang at it, oblivious to the strain. Before the judges could ring the bell, Buck had that squirrel in his grasp and that engine dangling from the lowest branch of an oak tree thirty feet into the woods.

That night they crowned Buck the national champion. He feasted on Old Roy and squirrel gravy. And in the morning, he started his new job: the West Virginia Highway Department wanted to see if Buck could pull Route 33 all the way to Washington before DC collapses. I don't know, that's a heavy task, even for Buck.

JONAH: THE REAL STORY

When I was growing up, I went to Sunday school and church pretty regular. I got to where I knew the Bible real good. I knew all about how Noah led the Egyptians out of Israel and how Moses built that ark and got all those animals and a bunch of two-by-twos on it. So I figured the best thing I could do was go to Divinity School.

Well, I was down there at Duke for a couple of years, and I'm here to tell you that them big-shot professors of religion got some mighty far-out things to teach you about the Bible. For example, I always thought AD meant "after dinner," seeing how the preacher man was always talking about the Last Supper, but down there at Duke, they told me it meant *amino domino,* or some such. And they say King James didn't write the Bible. In fact, it wasn't even written in English originally. It was written in some kind of language called Hebrew. Now, just between you and me, I always thought Hebrew was some kind of real man's beer, you know, "He-Brew for the He-Man beer drinker in your life!"

Now, it didn't take long before one of those professors assigned me a big paper to write. He told me I had to write a paper on the Book of Jonah, and well,

that's what this story is all about. You see, I got down
in the basement of Duke's library and came across a
long-forgotten book. It was dusty, and mice had sam-
pled the first few pages. As it turns out, Jonah wasn't
from the ancient Near East at all; in fact, he was from
right here in West Virginia. This is a story about
trains, giant fish, and West Virginia, and it comes
right out of the Bible, honest.

Ol' Jonah was sitting way up Nah holler one day.
He was on his front porch in an old rocking chair,
nestled between his refrigerator and his washing
machine. The sweet, melodious sounds of the *Andy
Griffith Show* were drifting through the open window.
Jonah had a He-Brew in one hand and was petting his
ever so gen-tile hound dog with his other hand.
Jonah was sitting there looking over his property. He
had a pile of tires on one side of his driveway and a
pile of self-milled lumber on the other. He smiled at
the rusted bed of a pickup he had converted into a
trailer; it had "Farm Use" spray-painted in sloppy
white letters across the side. A twinkle came to
Jonah's eye as he stared at the side of his shed, where
he had hung one hubcap from every GM car ever
made. He was thinking to himself, "West Virginia.
Almost Heaven."

Just then the Word of the Lord came to Jonah. The
Lord said, "Jonah, get up and get on over to
Halfdollar. A great evil has come up there, and they
need some revivaling!"

Well, Jonah had done some preaching in the past,
but lately he'd been doing a little backsliding, if you
know what I mean, and I expect you do. He didn't want
to go to Halfdollar, so he threw on his boots and headed toward Cowen, figuring to catch a train to Grafton.
Of course, you all know about Cowen, the depot for
that fine and famed run of Weirton's world-famous

steel fashioned into CS&X railroad tracks running clear from Cowen to Grafton via Burnsville, Buckhannon, Carrolton, and Philippi. Jonah knew full well that those trains ran directly away from Halfdollar, and he aimed to catch one despite the Lord's call. He got down in the bushes and waited for a train to pull out of the station.

Before long, a 168-car CS&X monster train loaded down with 19,364 tons of pure West Virginia bituminous coal started out. Jonah was fully aware of the fact that jumping trains is strictly illegal, so he looked over his left shoulder, then his right, and seeing that the coast was clear, he grabbed hold of the ladder on the last car of that train. He pulled himself into the coal, got comfortable, and fell asleep almost immediately. Running from the Lord, after all, tends to tire a man out.

That train had barely left the Cowen depot when a great storm kicked up. Most of you know those tracks run right alongside the mighty Buckhannon River, and as the rains fell, the river rose. Before long, the water was even with the rail bed, then with the timbers, then it was licking up over the tracks. The crew and the engineer were not happy with this turn of events. The engineer was an experienced man and had ridden out many a storm. He was in his favorite engine, on his favorite run of track; but by the time the water was above the wheels, the engineer was getting a little nervous. He and the crew both knew that, no matter how good they were, there was no way they were gonna get that train to float. The whole crew dropped to their knees and started praying to their various gods, but alas, Charlie Daniels and Richard Petty have little control over the weather.

The engineer climbed out of the engine and started walking across the top of the coal cars, wringing his hands in desperation. That's when he found Jonah, asleep like a pocket of methane in the coal. He reached down and picked Jonah up by his collar. He said, "Boy! You are in a lot of trouble. First of all, you're trespassing. Second, we're in a terrible fix here. The river's rising, and soon this train will be under-water."

Jonah looked at the engineer and calmly said, "Well, I got some good news, and I got some bad news. The bad news is that all this is my fault. God told me to go to Halfdollar, but I ran toward Grafton instead. The good news is, well, all you have to do to get out of this mess is let me off the train."

The engineer was a kind man; he took compassion on Jonah. It's the '90s after all, and men are much more in touch with their emotions; so the engineer hugged Jonah, held him in his arms, and promptly tossed him off the very next bridge they came to. Sure enough, the storm stopped and the water start-ed dropping, but Jonah plopped right into the Buckhannon River.

Below the spillway, as you all know, the Buckhannon River is a shallow, nasty, murky, sewage-fed river. But above the spillway, it's a deep, nasty, sewage-fed river full of the ugliest, meanest wildlife you've ever seen. It was into these waters that Jonah splashed.

Quicker than you can say "live bait to go," Jonah was swallowed up by the biggest, meanest, sewage-eating river carp south of the Ohio River. I can only assume that being in the belly of a river carp is some-thing like being locked in the bathroom of a cross-country Greyhound bus with two drunk sick pigs and Ted Kennedy. But Jonah was in the belly of that fish for three days before he ever started praying. I've been on dates that lasted only three minutes before I was praying, but Jonah held out.

Finally though, he said, "God, I admit it, it's all my fault. I ain't the smartest cuss you ever put on Earth. I mean, I did think that 'Hooked on Phonics' was a fishing lure, but I can see you're mad at me. I get the point with the storm and the train and the big, nasty fish and all. I guarantee you right now, Lord, if you get me out of this fish, I'll do anything you want. I swear."

The Lord heard Jonah's prayer and had compassion on him, and the Lord spoke to that fish. That carp swam toward the shore and spit Jonah out like so much chewed Beechnut. Jonah hit the bank kind of hard and rolled, but more than anything, his pride was hurt. He knew what he had to do, though. He got up, brushed himself off, and headed straight for Halfdollar, stopping only long enough to shower, play the Lotto, and try and satiate his strange but undeniable craving for sushi.

Wɪᴛʜ Gᴏᴅ As Mʏ Wɪᴛɴᴇss

A deserted, abandoned, forgotten, rusted, over-grown stretch of railroad tracks is not the same thing as a stretch of tracks that your best pal describes by saying, "With God as my witness, I swear I have never, ever, in all my life, seen a train on this stretch of tracks. We'll be fine. Come on. It'll be fun." The difference may sound subtle enough, even benign, but some things you must learn the hard way.

First of all, check your source, break the statement down, seek out the facts. For example, the statement "with God as my witness" is utterly meaningless to an atheist or an agnostic. Ask your yourself, "Have I ever known this guy to go to church?" Second, the statement "never, ever, in all my life" is rubbish under most circumstances but especially if your friend grew up in Maryland and you now are stand-ing way in the woods of West Virginia—a place your friend has never, ever, in all his life, been. You see, good friends will not lie to you, but they seldom will tell you the truth. And when they do tell you the truth, God help you.

All of this is to bring us to the point in the story where my buddy Paul said, "Let's take the subma-rine down to the river for a test drive," but that's no place to start a story either.

I can tell you right now that this is the sort of story that takes so long to get to the start of that it's nearly finished by the time you're halfway through but just starting by the time you hear the last word. So try and keep up; I'll take 'er slow.

Paul Drake is a man of Scottish heritage and stands every bit of five-foot-six. He has a red beard that looks like an Irish setter died under his nose and a head of hair that looks like half the fire ants in the world fighting, feuding, and otherwise getting drunk and stumbling just over Paul's eyes and all the way down his back. If he's not wearing greasy blue jeans and a black T-shirt, he is plumb naked. Either scenario is equally as likely.

Paul, quite by accident, discovered a picture of a submarine in the encyclopedia one day, but this was no average sub. In fact, this was one of the first submarines. Just briefly, because I hate too many facts in my stories, a guy named Bushnell built a sub he called the Turtle way back in 1776. With this submarine, Bushnell tried to sink British warships. The Turtle was essentially a large barrel with a hand-cranked propeller and a man-powered water pump. Bushnell went under British ships and tried to attach bombs to their hulls. The sub worked; the bombs didn't.

Anyway, seeing how it was the last semester of our senior year in college, and we each had no fewer than three papers due, lab projects to complete, foreign languages to learn, and tests to take, Paul decided the time was ripe to build a working replica of the Turtle in his dorm. I think it is safe to say that, of all the guys who lived on the third floor of our dorm that year, Paul was the only one with a shipyard in the middle of his floor.

Paul paid a couple of football players to lug an old heating oil tank up the three flights of stairs to his room. He then went home for the weekend and came back with his welding equipment. Soon there were two fifty-five-gallon drums affixed to the sides of the oil tank for ballast. Because the tank and the drums were gray, I told Paul the thing looked less like a submarine and more like three Siamese hippos joined at the ribs. At that, he became incensed. He found a can of pink paint in the garbage, and from then on the sub looked much more like two baby pigs suckling their mother. Paul even painted eyes and snouts. Still, out of reverence, he named his sub the Turtle II.

In all honesty, the creation of the Turtle II is a whole other story, but this does get us to the point of its launching, which brings us to the "with God as my witness" deserted tracks out toward French Creek. Now, don't be confused; these tracks were made from Weirton's world-famous steel, but they were not that fine and famed run stretching clear from Cowen to Grafton via Burnsville, Buckhannon, Carrolton, and Philippi. These tracks, supposedly, were deserted.

To save time and embarrassment, I will not go into how we got the sub out of the building, through the woods, and onto the tracks. I will say that the dean was not mad just because we blew a hole in one of the walls of our dorm, a hole just larger than the Turtle II, but also because the falling bricks and assorted shrapnel did a number on his new car. Of course, when the rope broke and the Turtle II plummeted the last ten feet—well, if the dean's car hadn't broken the fall, this story might just end there. There are days I wish it had. I further suspect that the dean would have been more at ease if we might have had the opportunity to calmly explain the whole incident in his office, perhaps over tea, rather than having to tell him about it while the Jaws of Life cut away the rest of his car from around his body. He was unhurt, but when he finally came around, he took the news poorly. I guess it was quite a shock to his system to see a giant mother pig, with two smaller pigs suckling, come blasting out of the wall of the dorm and then do a belly-flop on his car.

So there we were. Paul had checked the Department of Natural Resources' records and discovered the deepest section of the Buckhannon River, and to that point we now were headed. Realizing that the deepest section was way in the woods but accessible by railroad track, Paul had rigged the Turtle II with some old Yugo rims that hugged the tracks nicely. All we had to do was lift the Turtle II onto the tracks and push. Easy as pie, especially on "God as my witness"-deserted tracks.

Actually, the whole thing was going quite well. Paul had paid the same football players who had carried the heating oil tank up the stairs to unload the sub from the hood of the dean's car and then load it onto a trailer. We hauled the Turtle II to the railroad tracks behind a pickup, and the ballplayers lifted it onto the track for us. He and I just pushed it along. The football players drove the truck home for us.

Paul had brought along a couple of quarts of cheap motor oil, and every now and again we lubricated our makeshift train wheels. We made pretty good speed. The nice thing about railroad tracks is that, even in West Virginia, companies go to great pains to lay them flat. We could get up a good head of speed and then just jump on. It was a lot like riding a shopping cart down the aisles of a grocery store, except our mothers were not present to yell at us. Perhaps it would have been better if they had been present. In fact, now that I think about it, mothers should be required to spend a lot more time with their collegiate sons. If your mother cannot come with you to school, one should be assigned.

You see, if either Paul's or my mother had been around, we would not have been riding a submarine that looked like two little pigs suckling their mother, down railroad tracks, on wheels lubricated by forty-weight motor oil. It just wouldn't have happened. I doubt we even would have built the thing. I probably would have been in my room reading. I'll never forgive my mother for this.

What Paul and I were about to learn was not a valuable life lesson: it was just another indication that we were not very bright. That's what they call foreshadowing.

We got up a good head of speed and thought ourselves fortunate when we started down a slight incline. We both jumped aboard. The incline proceeded around a blind curve. Paul leaned down and lubricated the wheels. That's when I started thinking that these tracks sure didn't look abandoned. For one thing, they weren't rusty. Abandoned tracks—heck, all tracks—rust pretty quickly. Railroad tracks can get a fine coating of rust on them overnight if it rains a little, but a steady procession of trains keeps tracks rust-free. In fact, enough trains passing in one day will get tracks downright shiny. The tracks we were on shone in the summer sun like mirrors. Furthermore, deserted tracks always have weeds growing out of the gravel, and the ties generally are in the advance stages of rotting. No weeds, and I swear the ties were so new that I could smell the creosote. I started to raise these points with Paul when I heard the train whistle. I could hear Paul mumbling, "With God as my witness—"

The train was coming at us like a rabid rhino. It literally picked us up, changed our direction, and then shot us back down the tracks the way we had come like a billiard ball. We didn't make the curve but instead rocketed off the tracks and proceeded to gain altitude. The wheels, with their coating of oil, had burst into flames due to the extreme friction generated by our speed along the tracks. When Paul saw the flames, his face went pale.

"Bil," he said, "I never did drain the heating oil from this tank. Well, I drained most of it, but the rest just sort of sloshed around the bottom while I worked. Except for when I was welding, I never really worried all that much about it."

It was another case of sympathetic magic. No sooner did Paul say that then the propeller of a passing airplane clipped the underside of the heating oil tank. The oil streamed out and was readily ignited by the burning Yugo rims. Now we were not just two guys sitting on three airborne pigs: we were two guys hanging on for dear life to a rocket-propelled submarine.

I looked down and noticed we were flying over campus. West Virginia Wesleyan has a beautiful campus that is punctuated by a marvelous chapel. The chapel has a clock tower that reaches high into the sky. I knew it was our only chance. I took out my stainless steel, seventy-four-function Swiss Army knife, quickly pulled out the anchor, and heaved to. I then opened up the come-along and attached it to the anchor's chain. The anchor dropped straight down and wrapped around the bell tower nicely. Paul and I worked the come-along feverishly. As we shortened the chain, we made a series of revolutions around the tower, slowing with each turn. When we slowed to a reasonable speed and were pointed in a safe direction, we let go of the come-along and shot off the tower like the stone out of David's sling.

In all honesty, I feel a little bad for the dean. You could see the shock on his face pretty clearly as we plunged out of the sky, straight toward his office window. Paul was waving his hat around and kicking the Turtle II like a bronco. To the dean we must have looked just like that scene in *Dr. Strangelove* when the guy rides the A-bomb out of the plane. As we crashed through the window, the snout of the pig caught the dean square in the chest. He flew backward as Paul and I flew forward into his office. The Turtle II, still looking like three pigs, was lodged in the window frame.

"Dean," Paul said as he stood up, "it's nice to see you again." Evidently the dean was pleased to see us as well because he went to his desk and pulled out two diplomas. He filled them out right there in his office and handed them to us. He said we hereby were excused from the rest of the year, provided we would go home right away. It was rather thoughtful of him.

My parents were quite proud. The incident solved an argument between them, too. You see, Mom always said I would graduate, but Dad said he did not believe I would graduate until pigs flew. I guess I proved him right.

THE SEVENTH SECOND

My friends and I attended and studied at West Virginia Wesleyan College in Buckhannon, West Virginia. Well, to be perfectly honest, mostly we just attended West Virginia Wesleyan. You see, not far from our school, there was a railroad tunnel that a man could climb up into and watch the trains pass by on the tracks below. Now, I say a man could do this because no woman would ever be stupid enough to.

At any rate, it was last April and going on noon when Paul, Steven, and myself all rolled out of our respective beds. Seeing as we all had class at 12:30, we figured it was the perfect time to take a hike. By class time, we were lying belly down thirty feet above Weirton's world-famous steel fashioned into CS&X railroad tracks running clear from Cowen to Grafton via Burnsville, Buckhannon, Carrolton, and Philippi. Now, we'd done this sort of thing before, so when we saw the signal go green and heard the train whistle in the distance, we didn't think twice about it. Then, to our horror, we heard a sonic boom and looked down just in time to see General Chuck Yeager at the controls of the lead engine of that CS&X monster train passing at Mach one beneath us.

When that train hit that tunnel going Mach one,

that tunnel became a vacuum Ol' Mr. Hoover could only dream of. Stuff was sucked in one end of that tunnel and blown out the other. I'm talking about sticks, rocks, trees, outhouses, train trestles—fact is, I ain't seen so much crap blown so fast since the last presidential campaign. I just looked down and said, "Eureka!"

It was quite a spectacle for about three seconds, but then the rafter I was lying on gave way, and folks, I found myself stuck to the last car of that train like a fly to paper. But that ain't the half of it 'cause the minute that train left the tunnel, the vacuum quit, and I was sliding down toward the tracks below.

I managed to flip myself around and grab hold of the rear axle of that train. I was flapping out like the tail on a kite, but the lift was leaving me quick, and I knew my feet soon would be dragging. It was a classic between-a-rock-and-a-hard-place situation, and I figured there were only two things I could do: I could either pull out my whip, lash it to those engines, and pull myself up like ol' cousin Indiana Jones, or I somehow could clamber up into that coal car. Now, pulling out my whip didn't seem very safe, so I reached in my pocket and pulled out my stainless steel, seventy-four-function Swiss Army knife and pulled open the harpoon gun and grappling hook. I quickly lashed a one-handed bowline around myself and two half hitches around the grappling hook. Then I fired that hook up into the coal car.

My arms were tired from holding myself out like ol' cousin Superman, so it took me three or four seconds to finally clamber up that rope into that coal car and to burrow a hole from the blasting wind into the bituminous coal. I took a deep breath and said, "Phew." I knew we must have been nearing my old friend Frank Androczi's Little Hungary Winery by then, so for the first time during the whole trip, I opened my eyes.

Lord, have mercy. The tracks behind me turned bright red and melted away. The creosoted ties burst into flames. The trees alongside the tracks pulled themselves out of the ground, and the mighty Buckhannon River swelled up into a forty-foot tidal wave. At the rate we were moving, I guess I was pretty lucky I hadn't lost my hat.

Honestly now, I enjoy a train ride as much as the next man, but until you've gone Mach one in a coal car on an Appalachian line, you may not understand my next move. I decided to get off that train. At first I figured to jump, but then it occurred to me that the laws of physics say that if the train was going Mach one, when I hit the ground I'd be going Mach one too, and I wasn't wearing my running shoes! I had an idea.

I scrambled down the ladder of that coal car as quickly as I could and picked up all the leaves, reeds, sticks, and garbage I could reach (course the garbage was out-of-state stuff) and put all that in my work-shop. Then I scrambled down that ladder one more time, hooked up an electric turbine engine off the wheels of that train, and ran the wires to the sewing machine on my knife. I ducked back in the car just in time not to be seen by the CS&X police in my home-town of Philippi.

Now, you all know about Philippi. That's where the covered bridge is that started the whole darn Civil War. Well, I knew that train was bound for Grafton and would be stopping there. And I knew the CS&X train cops would be waiting there to arrest me for trespassing. Furthermore, I knew Grafton was only fourteen miles from Philippi, and I wanted to know just how much time I had to work. I pulled out my calculator and punched fourteen miles into Mach one. I discovered I'd be in Grafton pretty darn quick.

I had to get off that train, so I set to work. From the leaves I'd grabbed, some of the refuse, and my very own T-shirt, I was able to weave a lightweight, nylon-type material, primitive though it was; and I sewed that into a huge hot air balloon. With some berries I'd picked I was able to dye that balloon a delicate shade of purple. Then I took the sticks and reeds and made a basket. I shredded my jeans and connected the basket to the balloon.

I was halfway through the fusion engine I was going to use to power my balloon when I remembered just how messy uranium is. "Besides," I figured, "I got all this wonderful West Virginia coal." But make no mistake; before I used that coal, I built a scrubber and scrubbed that coal to get all the sulfates out so I wouldn't pollute the air of the greatest state in the Union, West Virginia. All that took nearly six seconds, and well, on the seventh second I rested.

While I was resting, I read a little Aristotle for a class, and then I made a diamond by squeezing a piece of coal between my thumb and forefinger. I attribute that ability mostly to the adrenaline rush. Soon I spotted a clearing. I quickly christened that balloon the West Virginia Flying America, tightened my goggles, threw my scarf around my neck, and when I got to that clearing, I just sort of lifted up and drifted off back to Buckhannon.

All in all, it was a darn exciting trip, and if any of you are coal miners, I thank you for the coal. It keeps America flying.

SECTION 3

PAUL

Carp in the Garden of Eden

Undoubtedly, it is difficult for a carp to understand man and even harder for him to understand woman. Fortunately for the carp, he has no need and makes no effort to understand either. Instead, he avoids both with equal effort.

Likewise, it is difficult to conceive of a woman understanding a carp. Fortunately for her, she has no desire to understand a carp and usually avoids him with the same effort he avoids her. As for the understanding of man, again, she has little desire. She generally finds it easier to conform or reform him to best suit her needs.

Man and misfortune enter the picture at the same time. Man endeavors to understand them both and usually fails as miserably at understanding the one as the other. He spends many sleepless nights on the riverbank trying to understand women and many sleepless nights in bed trying to understand carp. This misfortune can be traced all the way back to poor Adam in the Garden of Eden, where it all began.

It seems as though Adam was strolling through the garden one afternoon, looking for bad habits to pick up, when he chanced upon a sewer pipe leading into the river. Peering into the murky water, Adam beheld the first carp. Somehow, he knew just what to do. Hastily inventing the fishhook, Adam tied it to a length of twenty-pound test mono-vine, baited it with some fresh corn, and became a fisherman.

Soon Adam was spending all his time down by the river, as fishermen are prone to do. Unfortunately, Adam was still a farmer, and that takes a lot of time too. Before long the garden was a weed bed, and the Big Boss was not pleased. So, the Boss went looking for Adam, and of course, found him on the riverbank.

"Hey, Adam, can I talk to you?"

"Not right now, Boss, I think I'm gettin' a bite."

The Boss shook his head and was forced to create the first snarl in Adam's vine. While Adam was busy untangling the vine—and creating profanity—the Boss continued.

"Look, Adam, we're getting behind schedule here. The garden is a wreck, and you haven't hoed a row this week."

"Well, Boss, I thought we'd just let it grow on its own—you know, nature's way."

"Adam, I am Nature, and my way is for you to get up there and weed that thing. Got it?"

"OK, OK, you don't have to get grouchy. Look, I'll get back at it just as soon as I catch the world record, all right?"

"What's the world record, Adam?"

"Sixty-two pounds, thirteen ounces."

"And what's your record?"

"Nine pounds even."

"Look, Adam, here's the deal: I can't wait that long, but I can't keep watching you either. I thought we could avoid this, but I guess not. Adam, I'm going to have to create Woman."

"Oh no! Not that. Anything but that, Boss! What's Woman?"

"Just don't you worry about that. She'll see you don't spend all your time down here. Yes sir, she'll fix your wagon."

"I don't even have a wagon. Listen, we'll just forget the whole thing. I'll make one more cast and then go up to work for a little while, OK?"

"Sorry, Adam, too late. But you'll be OK. Woman has a lot of advantages too."

"Like what, Boss?"

"I'll make her pretty to look at."

"How 'bout I work three hours a day and you just send me her picture?"

"No deal. But she has other qualities too. With Woman around, you won't have to catch the world record; you can just lie about it."

"What's a lie, Boss?"

"See, Adam, I told you you need Woman. She'll fill you in on that one after she creates it. Why don't you just take a little nap and we'll talk about it later?"

Well, Adam took a little nap, and the next thing he knew, there was Woman nagging him to get up and tidy her garden. Her garden! And sure enough, Woman saw to it that Adam kept the garden neat, and she made sure he didn't go fishing until all his work was done. In fact, she saw to it that he did all sorts of chores that he really didn't see any need for.

It only took a few days for Adam to see that this was just too much. He decided to go find the Boss and file a complaint, so off he went. As he passed by the river on the way to the Boss' office, there was that Woman, swimming in his fishing hole!

"Now just look here, Woman!" he shouted. "You get up out of that water this instant. You're scaring my carp!"

He sounded so mad that Woman obeyed him and climbed out. Now, fig leaves were not too effective as swimwear, and the woman climbed out of the water and the fig leaves at the same time. Suddenly Adam wasn't nearly so angry. In fact, he forgot he was angry at all. And when Woman decided to let Adam in on a few more of her advantages, why, Adam decided that maybe there were other ways to relax than fishing.

So things settled down in the garden, and the years passed by. Sometimes Adam went fishing when his work was through, and sometimes he even caught his limit. And sometimes he stayed home when the work was through. And when Woman created the lie, Adam picked it up and began telling astounding fishing tales. But he never told Woman that he had caught the world record because he was afraid she'd make him stop going fishing.

Then one day, when Adam was very old, the Boss stopped by the house. They sat together, watching the game and sipping a couple of cold ones. The Boss said, "Adam, I guess it's about time for you to retire from the garden. I guess you'll go back to fishing all the time and won't be needing that Woman any-more, so I'll just take her back."

"What do you mean, 'You guess you'll take her back?' What am I supposed to do without her?"

"Why, Adam, you're the guy who didn't want her in the first place."

"That was before I met her."

"But you just told me the other day that you don't understand her, didn't you?"

"Of course, and I don't, but I bet you don't either."

"So?"

"So, it's like this, Boss. She's always making me do stuff I don't want to do, and she yells at me for no reason—well, usually for no reason—but that doesn't mean I don't want her around, you know. Besides the carp, she's all I got, and even fishing wouldn't be all that good if there weren't someone to act like they believed my stories. I guess there are a whole lot of things in the world that I don't understand, but I don't think there is anything more fun or more important not to understand than a woman. And carp."

And the Boss said, "Adam, I believe you're right."

THE CARPMAN'S CREED

Of all the chapters of the Brotherhood of the Fin, none is so fine and pure as the Carpclub. This fact is exemplified by the code all true carpers swear and live by. The oath, which is to be sworn upon the banks of a muddy ol' river, is taken by placing the casting hand on a six-pack and the other hand behind the back with the index and middle fingers crossed.

"I, (state your name), do solemnly swear:

- To never cause undue injury to any carp, using utmost care in hooking my fish, and keeping it out of the water only long enough for everyone to see it.

- To never weigh or measure any carp with reliable scales, which action might leave emotional scars upon smaller fish, but instead to make an honest estimation of its huge size to the best of my ability.

- To never set the drag on my reel lighter than necessary to make it scream at the slightest nibble or at the weight of my sinkers.

- To never play a snag like a big fish to impress passing boaters.

- To never round off to an "even dozen" any fewer than seven carp.
- To never kick my partner's rod when he isn't looking to make him think he's getting a bite.
- To never kick my partner, no matter how many nor how big the carp he catches.
- To try and limit the size of "the one that got away" to a length of not more than four feet and weight of not more than thirty-five pounds, unless it was obviously bigger.
- To always reveal to all fellow carpmen the exact locations of hotspots (give or take a county).
- To try not to laugh at trouters who brag about four-pound "monsters."

Naturally, given that the art of carp angling is one of adaptability, certain rules may be modified from time to time as circumstances require, providing strict procedural guidelines are followed. In order for an amendment to be deemed proper, the amending angler must:
a) Lie like hell, and
b) Get away with it.

WALLEYED SUCKERS
AND WATERDOGS

6

I met Rebus Ward the same day I met my wife. It was the first day of the eighth grade, and they were at the bus stop when I got there. It would be twelve more years before I married and began to get in trouble with my wife. Rebus and I did not need that long (to get in trouble, not to get married—we weren't like that).

Rebus, I learned, was just as fanatical about fishing as I was. Over the years to come, we would spend countless hours talking about fishing, reading about fishing, watching fishing shows on TV, ordering fishing gear from catalogs, and of course, just plain fishing. We fished for anything that swam. We fished anywhere we could get to by walking, riding bikes, or bumming rides from adults. Naturally, most of our trips were local. The trips I remember best, though, were the ones we made a couple of times a year to the Wards' cabin at Claytor Lake in Radford, Virginia.

Mornings at Claytor Lake were a time-honored tradition for Rebus and me. They began at precisely four A.M., when Rebus would leap from bed, fully dressed, and make breakfast. It did not take long to unwrap Twinkies and pour hot tap water over instant coffee. He would bring me my coffee in bed and then kick and tug at me until I, too, was out of bed. Because most of the first cup of coffee usually spilled into my nose and ears while Rebe rousted me from the sack, I always was glad that the art of making water boil was not among his culinary skills.

When I gained full consciousness, we would bolt down the Twinkies and chase them with more warm coffee. Once nourished, I would bite off a chew of Brown's Mule plug tobacco, Rebe would stuff in a pinch of snuff, then we'd both light a big cigar and head for the side porch. We'd play a quick game of pool on a very unlevel table and cement the day's fishing plans.

On one such occasion, a fine, crisp, April dawn, we both expressed a gut feeling that the Little River was the place to pursue our quarry that day. Rebus' dad, Rebus, who was not a fisherman, was always of the opinion that our gut feelings more likely were attributed to the Twinkie and tobacco breakfasts than to any great angling intuition. Rebus Sr. also felt sure that there were things in life more important than fishing. Rebe and I felt he should keep opinions like that to himself, and we said as much too—but only when old Rebus was not around.

At any rate, the car was loaded, and we were off to the riverbank that morning. The Little River is a very aptly named stream that flows into the New River just below Claytor Dam. The small, picturesque dam is just a few hundred yards above the mouth of the Little River. Water surging over the dam has scoured out a pool about a hundred yards around and about eight feet deep. A fine mist drifts over the dam, creating thousands of tiny rainbows on a sunny day. The banks and river bottom are strewn with large boulders that keep the swift current white and boiling.

On this day, we arrived just at sun-up. We refreshed our chaws and leisurely surveyed the scene. We discussed lure selection and techniques. As was our strict policy at the lake, we used only artificial lures during daylight hours, except under extreme circumstances, like when the fish weren't biting on them. I tied on a brand new lure and set off confidently downstream, assured by the package that I soon would be getting "more bumps, taps, bites, and strikes" than I ever "thought possible."

Rebus took more time setting up because he was putting into action, for the first time, his brand new ultralight rod and reel. The reel was a beauty, the most expensive one either of us ever had owned. It was especially dear to Rebus because of all the suffering and sacrifice he had endured to buy it. We always had been about the same height and weight, right up until the fateful day when Rebe first saw that reel in K-Mart. We still are about the same height, but to this day I outweigh him by about twenty pounds, all due to that reel. He decided he had to have it, and as an eighth-grader, his only source of cash was the thirty-five cents Mrs. Ward gave him each day for school lunch.

Every school day for five months he put one dime and one quarter in his piggy-bank (Rebe was the only eighth-grader I knew who still owned and operated a real piggy-bank). His only lunch during that whole time was what he could bribe off me with promises that I could use the reel a few times. Because of my contributions, I was almost as proud as he the day we strode up to the sports counter at K-Mart and Rebe plunked down a sweatsock, to the clerk's horror, that was filled with exactly 180 quarters and 110 dimes, with which he purchased that shiny, navy blue masterpiece.

Anyway, Rebe lovingly rigged up this outfit. His next task was to find a suitable lure to honor this occasion. He chanced upon a handsome little crawdad jig, which he secured to his two-pound test line with a clench knot. Ready for action, he strolled to the foot of the dam. It was considered a good omen to catch a fish on the first cast with a new rod. For this reason, I had allowed Rebe uncontested use of the best spot on the whole stretch. To reach the spot, he had to leap about four feet across a deep, swift channel to reach a rock in the water. Footing was good there during the day, and it was worth the risk to jump because this hole consistently yielded redeyes, bluegill, suckers, and feisty smallmouths.

Ceremoniously, Rebus Ward made the virgin cast. The jig arched out over the water and gently plopped down. The reaction that followed was so abrupt and unexpected that the rod nearly flew from his hands. Something large had solidly taken the jig! The tiny rod doubled and appeared to be looking for a way to triple, and the miniature reel screamed like a witch in holy water. Rebe's eyes bugged. Whatever had hold of his lure dove to the bottom and began doing laps around the hole. I raced over the jagged rocks to help my pal. There was no need.

After a minute, the thing on the other end tired of the game and, with a savage jerk, parted the line. We never even saw it. I coaxed my buddy off the rock and over to some shade. After a few Oreo cookies and a dip of snuff, his voice returned.

"Well, Possum," he said. (Rebus always called me Possum, which was short for Possumhead. It was a name he made up for me, although I don't know why. It was not due to any personal resemblance.)

"I'll be derned. All the way up from the main river, and this early in the season too. Ain't never seen one up here so early before. Have you?"

"Seen what, Rebus?"

"Hippo, Possum. That was a hippopotamus, dead certain. No denying it, that's what it was. And so early in the season too."

There most certainly was denying it, I thought to myself, but I did not say so out loud. Experiences like these can be very trying to the victim. Gradually, Rebus returned to his old self, and fishing resumed. The only permanent damage done by this incident was that Rebe decided he needed a rod that could handle anything up to a hippo and immediately started saving for it. He was a junior in college before he ever ate another school lunch. Mrs. Ward still wonders why her boy is so thin.

Toward evening, a large school of suckers moved in and began to hit on anything we threw out to them. We decided to keep track of how many we could catch, so we broke out the stringer. By dark we had about fifty of those big ugly critters on the line. We decided to take a picture. Actually, we took two, one of each of us holding the suckers up in the fading light. The result was a couple of dark silhouettes of us holding up a big, bulky stringer of large, undefinable fish.

"Almost look like walleyes, don't they, Possum? Why, in that light you can't hardly tell the..." His voice trailed off, our eyes met sinisterly, and we broke into evil grins.

"Yup, Rebus, that's the most walleyes we've ever caught in one day."

"It sure is, Poss. Sure is a good thing we took these pictures before the stringer broke and they all got away," he said as he began tossing suckers back into the water.

"And if that turtle hadn't gotten into them, we might have saved a few," I said. "But these things happen."

Being the dedicated anglers we were, it did not bother us a bit to pass that tale on to the Ward household the next day. They took it hook, line, and sinker. All of them but wise old Grampa Damon. He took one look at those pictures and said, "Walleyes? Hell those look like a bunch of damn—" (At this point Rebe slyly slid the old-timer a brew. Grampa, who was on a strict beer ration under Grandma's watchful eye, took the beer, slid it under the couch cushion, and re-evaluated the picture.) "—like a bunch of damn nice walleyes!"

Meanwhile, night had fallen, and we returned to the river. Out came our minnows, nightcrawlers and crawdads. Out came the heavy rods and big hooks. We built a fire, propped the rods on some forked sticks, and propped our feet on the rocks. This always was a relaxed time with the occasional carp or catfish to keep us alert. I was enjoying the calm, but Rebe's new reel still was calling him.

He informed me that he had to go back up to the rock and make a few more casts. I told him I would stay and watch the other rods. I also warned him to be careful because after dark that rock got slick from the mist coming off the dam.

I had just rebaited a hook when I heard his yell.

"Poss-UM-blumph!"

"Blumph?" I thought as I hastily reeled in all our lines. (No emergency is so great as to risk having an unattended rod stolen by a fish.) I reached the rock, but my partner was nowhere to be seen. I searched the bank and called, but still no luck. And then I saw it.

Sticking six inches straight out of the water was the delicate butt of Rebus Ward's new ultralight rod, with the brand new reel attached, still high and dry above the froth and foam between the bank and the rock. I leaned over, grasped the rod, and heaved. Up came the rod with Rebus attached to the top guide by two fingers. He was choking and sputtering, and his lips were bright blue. As soon as his mouth cleared the water, he gasped, "Did it get wet? Did my new reel touch the water?"

As I dragged him to the fire, I assured him it had not. I built the fire to a roaring blaze, and in a few minutes he was engulfed in a hissing cloud of steam. His color began to return and his lip soon bulged with that familiar snuff bulge.

"Jeez, that was a close one, Possum. If'n that water had been six inches deeper, that could have been disaster, you know?"

You always can tell a true angler by his devotion to his tackle. Give a good fisherman a fine rod and reel to hold, then throw him over a cliff. Know what you'll see? You can bet your last dollar that you'll see a man bouncing off trees and rocks, all the while shifting that rod from hand to hand to save it from a single bump or scratch. When he hits the bottom, ask him why. His simple answer likely will be very much along the lines of, "Hell, son, bones heal, rods don't!" Such a man was Rebus Ward.

I left my friend at the fireside and cast out all the rods again. Rebus fumbled about behind me and managed to spill his tackle box. Rebe's tackle box was more of a crate, one of those huge, multi-drawered affairs the professional bass fishermen use in tournaments. It had about 2700 compartments, and he was highly proud of it. Santa Claus had given it to him the past Christmas. I was about to help him reload it, but I began to have a problem of my own.

My bait seemed to be rising in the water. The current

was swift, so I was using a big sinker. The weight had held the bait on the bottom all night, and I could not figure out why suddenly it would not stay down. I called Rebe over, and we both watched in silence. Finally I set the hook. We heard a splash, but the line was dead.

I'm an outdoorsman. I've seen strange sights and heard strange sounds at night before—you know, bats, spiders, snakes, and the like. Heck, I've even been followed by UFOs, and once a whole herd of Bigfeet tracked me for more than an hour before I gave them the slip. Still and all, what I saw next made my skin crawl and my hair stand on end. My bait, by all indications of the angle of the line, now had risen—*above the water line*!! Instinctively, I set the hook, hard. SPLASH!

"Hot dog! Ya got him now!" Rebe yelled.

"Yeah," I gulped. I reeled hard. There was little resistance, but something was on the line and coming in fast. Rebus knelt to help land it. I yelled at him, but it was too late.

If it is possible to freeze for one heartbeat, Rebus Ward did it then, his hand outstretched, only inches from the gaping, hissing jaws, the bulging eyes, and the flat head with the blood-red feathery gills. Then Rebe erupted. With a terrified scream, he leapt about five feet off the ground, turned in midair, and as far as I can tell, flew the twenty yards to the car without ever touching the ground. He dove in and locked the doors.

Since this thing was attached to my line, I could not pursue this option. I guided it over to the fire-light. As I got a better look, I recognized it. It was a mud puppy or, as they are called locally, a waterdog. I had seen pictures of them in *National Geographic*. Well, I'd seen hippos in *National Geographic* too, but I no more expected to see a waterdog on my line than I had expected Rebe to believe he had seen a hippo on his line earlier.

I did the only macho thing that could be done. I mashed it with a rock. I coaxed Rebus out of the car, and we stood there, looking at the thing. Suddenly, Rebus let out a war whoop and began a wild kind of dance, leaping, howling, and tearing off his clothes.

"Now what?" I snapped.

"I...I...I...," he stuttered. "I was in the water with that thing!"

"Cut it out, Rebus!" I yelled. "It's dead."

He did not quit until he stood naked in the firelight. "Whew," he sighed, "I was sure some of those nasty things had snuck into my clothes. Reckon not though, huh?" He said sheepishly.

"Come on, let's call it a night," I told him.

"Fine by me. My system couldn't take another shock, Possum."

We gathered up our gear. Rebe reached for his tackle box by the fire. I guess it was a little too close to the flames because as he lifted it, one whole square-yard side just dropped off, plumb melted.

"Good thing I had this gunnysack in the trunk," I said to myself as I poured Rebus Ward into it.

Lightning Bugged

We mountaineers have long suffered the stereo-typical image of being uneducated hillbillies on the front porch, bare feet a-swingin', hooterin' fresh white lightnin' from mason jars with our trusty, rusty squirrel guns at arm's reach. My cousins—Matt (the lawyer) and Paul Tim a.k.a. PT, (the doctor)—and I (B.S. in Public Trust from Honest Aldo's Auto Emporium and University) were discussing the tragedy of such prejudices as we sat on the porch of Uncle Bill's (PhD, chemist) Jackson County farmhouse in the middle of three hundred acres of prime woods and meadow. It was the eve of fall turkey season.

We concluded smugly that we were the very antithesis of that stereotype. OK, we were barefoot on the porch, but all other similarities ended there. We were smoking very aristocratic long-stemmed clay pipes and sipping a well-aged local rye served from a hand-blown Blenco decanter with matching glasses. There were no ancient firearms about, either. Matt sported a Weatherby Mark V rifle with gold inlays and a Leopold scope. PT was casually working the action of his Russian Kalishnikov 7.65 mm sniper rifle, the one he had acquired while in residency as a Peace Corps volunteer in Afganistan. I was toying

with the fully automatic Hecler & Koch MP5 subma-
chine gun I borrowed from the South Charleston
Police Department for such occasions. I consider it
possibly the finest small game and varmint rifle ever
produced. The thought of the outside world considering us "hicks" was almost enough to drive us to
jump into Matt's BMW and shoot up some deer-
crossing signs on I-77. Naturally, our civility pre-
vailed. We held a farting contest instead.

It was not without reason that we were so armed.
Our quarry for the next day—the native Jackson
County wild turkey—is one of the most elusive and
cunning species of game on the face of the earth.
Were it not for the folks at Butterball, pigs from
Parkersburg to Ripley would have been mighty nervous come Thanksgiving. If the Pilgrims had sailed
up Mud Run and landed in Ravenswood instead of
stopping at Plymouth Rock, crow with oyster dress-
ing might be a whole lot more popular in America
today. The basic fact is those bearded birds are good.
They're crafty and sneaky and, year after year, take no
mercy on us as we futilely attempt to fill them with
lead and stuffing, in that order.

There was only one logical, satisfactory reason we
had never bagged one of them. It was not a scarcity
of turkeys. As we sat on the porch that evening, we
could hear them, as always, clucking and gobbling to
each other from across the ridges and hollows of the
farm as they settled in for the night. It was not a
result of our not knowing the territory. We three had
spent a good deal of our youth hiking, camping, and
exploring those three hundred acres. We knew it like
the backs of our hands. Our marksmanship was not to
blame either. George Washington once commented
that, with an army of men from the hills of Vandalia,
he could lick the world, or something to that effect,

and it is well known that he was not a man prone to exaggeration. As the descendants of those men from those hills, we all were crack shots. No, it was obvious to us where the fault lay: it was the turkeys—they cheated.

As the shadows grew long, and darkness settled over the farm, we quietly smoked and took in the solitude of the country evening. Sounds of the night drifted to our ears—the clinking of dishes as Aunt Arlene made her famous sweet rolls in the kitchen, the call of the whippoorwill from deep in the woods, the taunts of those damn turkeys roosted high in the trees. A mantle of peace enveloped the farm like a warm, soft blanket against the cold, hurrying world about us. It was...boring.

The silence was shattered by the booming report of a high-powered rifle—a report that bounded across the valleys, echoed from the hilltops, and sent dozens of unseen small critters dashing for cover on the forest floor. Matt leaned back in his chair and calmly ejected a spent cartridge from his gun.

"Got 'im," he said.

"Got who?" his brother wanted to know.

"I just shot a lightning bug off that walnut tree," Matt said proudly.

"Was he flying or just sitting there?" PT asked suspiciously.

"He was sitting."

"Uh huh, just as I figured. I'll bet he was lit up, too, wasn't he?"

"Well, yeah, of course he was lit. What of it?" Matt asked, some of the wind noticeably slipping from his sails.

"Oh, nothing," PT replied, "except that anyone could hit a sitting, lit firefly. That's why it's illegal, ain't it, Paul?"

"That's right," I agreed. "It's right there in the books. Right next to the part about not squishing praying mantises or ladybugs."

Matt's smile faded as he became defensive. "All right," he said, "I suppose that one of you smarty-pants can tell me just how it is that you can shoot one of 'em?"

"Sure," PT replied. "Flying."

"And dark," I added.

Matt wanted to be shown. PT jacked a three-inch shell into the sniper rifle, licked his thumb and wetted the front sight, and put the rifle to his shoulder. We watched him as he scoured the darkness. Suddenly, about forty feet out and to the right, a bug lit up. PT swung into action, the tip of his barrel dipping as he tracked the invisible insect's course. He fired. Thirty-five feet out, a little to the left, the bug's cover was blown. Like a tiny Roman candle in the blackness, so was that bug as he plummeted to the earth in a shower of cold, phosphorous sparks.

Matt was visibly impressed. George Washington would have loved it. Uncle Bill, attracted by the shots, joined us on the porch. He inquired about our activities, and we filled him in. It just happened that he had done some extensive research on cold light while working at the South Charleston Union Carbide Tech Center, so he was an expert on lightning bugs. We boys were interested in not catching heck for shooting so late, so we listened as he delivered a long dissertation on the subject. It was a bit too technical for us, but we nodded our heads in what we hoped was an intelligent manner and tried to look thoughtful. Hunters are early risers, though, and after an hour of the impromptu lesson, we excused ourselves and went to bed, leaving Uncle Bill making Chinese-looking symbols on a paper napkin as he diagramed the formula.

We arose two hours before dawn, donned camouflage clothes, and painted our faces black. We talked in hushed whispers as we checked our guns and ate sticky buns with sassafras tea. With all due respect to your grandmother, no one makes a finer homemade sweet roll than Aunt Arlene. With several dozen of them in our bellies, we headed out, armed to the teeth, to match wits with the turkeys.

In the bottom, over the hill from the house, stands an old barn. The meadow around it, fertilized by the droppings of domestic stock long gone to the great deep-freeze, is rich with wildflowers and weeds. Here, in the early morning hours, the turkeys gather to feast on grasshoppers. We slithered on our stomachs, becoming soaked with dew, in the dark before dawn, to lie in ambush for those feathered masters of deceit.

Dawn broke; we heard them coming in. They joked and cajoled as they sauntered down. While the first rays of sunlight filtered through the briers and brambles on the ridge tops, we three hunters scarcely could believe our luck. It appeared as though a great turkey jamboree was about to take place. Toms with beards down to their hambone-sized drumsticks strutted about. Hens with more white meat on their breast than Dolly Parton bobbed and scratched around. The sight was every turkey hunter's dream come true.

I lined my sights on a forty-pound tom. He looked up and stared me straight in the eye. My finger tightened on the trigger...and the tom just disappeared! I shook my head and rubbed my eyes, and just as quickly, the bird reappeared. I tried it again, but with the same results: the bird faded out just as I got ready to shoot.

I glanced over at PT, who had a fine hen in his crosshairs. I watched his knuckle tighten on his trigger, and then he looked back at the turkey. As with mine, just as PT began to fire, the turkey vanished. We looked at Matt, who lay prone with his fine rifle aimed dead at another gobbler. He hitched his shoulder and squeezed. Déjà vu. No bird.

We rose in the wet grass. The normally flighty, wary birds barely bothered to hurry as they filed out of the field. We stood shaking our heads in wonder as we surveyed the scene. A rumpled piece of paper caught my eye. I knelt to pick it up. It was a soggy napkin, and I unfolded it as Matt and PT gathered round. Though the ink had bled and the figures had blurred, it was painfully obvious what the document was: Uncle Bill's scratch sheet from the previous night's lecture.

Our security had been breached. As we had confidently talked among ourselves the night before, we'd been under turkey surveillance. They'd witnessed the firefly incident and taken notes. They had been lurking in the shadows as Uncle Bill spoke, and the talk that had gone over our heads went straight to their hearts. We'd been infiltrated. Technically fowled. Lightning bugged.

You see, with the info they had gathered and the formulas they had stolen, those turkeys had mastered the theories and principles of cold light. Down from the trees they came, en masse, to gorge on lightning bugs. With their gizzards stuffed full, they gathered in the thickets and synchronized themselves, alternately blacking out and then beaming forth light, until they could turn themselves on and off at will. Then, like peacocks, they had strutted into the meadow, confident in their treacherous plan. As we scoped them in, they simply had turned themselves out, invisible to the naked eye—the stealth turkeys of Jackson County.

Hillbillies? Fine, call us what you will, but when

you run up against squirrels tapping your phone lines or deer stockpiling nuclear armaments, you'll know whom to call. We've seen that sort of thing. And if a Thanksgiving ever comes that you need a good recipe for roasted crow, give us a ring. We're pretty good at that dish. Our turkeys have made us eat it enough times.

No Stranger to Trouble

You might not know it to look at me, but I'm no stranger to trouble. My momma always said trouble was like a box of chocolates with me: she never did know when I was going to get into it. It still seems like every time I turn around, trouble is sneaking up behind me and biting me square on the buttocks. It's worse than a treble hook on a toilet seat in a one-hole outhouse.

Take two weeks ago Tuesday, for example. I was at work when my musical pal David Morris stopped by. He was booking his next world tour (it must have a Disney theme 'cause it's a small, small world tour). He said he had to take a fox up to Weirton, and when I asked why he had to take a fox to Weirton, he said he didn't rightly know. All Dave knew was that a guy in Weirton wanted some information on the tour and asked Dave to send him a fox. Actually, the guy wanted Dave to send the fox through a fox machine, but Dave didn't have no fox machine, and even if he did, he didn't reckon he could get that fox into it. It was a pretty suspicious type of fox.

I was needing to get to Weirton for some time to stop in at Weirton Steel, where they custom cast the twenty-pound stainless steel, slip-sliding sinkers that I use on my Monster Stick. It's got that whole reel full of fifty-pound test Stren carp cord. It's the castingest outfit I own, and a couple of split shots from K-Mart just won't do the trick. I asked Dave if I could go along, and he said, "Sure." We climbed into his big, purple, musician-type touring van, and off we went.

It started out pretty good. I got the sinkers, and Dave, well Dave gave that guy so much information he said we could keep the fox after all. It was long after dark, darker than the inside of a cow, when we headed back. We were south bound on I-79. There at Morgantown, where I-68 comes in from Maryland, we got behind a big truck. And that's when the fox started acting funny.

First he started sniffing the air and whimpering a bit. The next thing we knew he started yipping and barking and hopping around. We were half afraid he had the hydrophobia and that was why the man gave him back to us. And then he done the strangest thing I ever saw a fox do. All of a sudden, he went on point, right straight at that truck in front of us. I took a closer look and noticed a sign that I hadn't noticed before. The sign on the back of that truck read, "Caution: Live Catfish."

Well, now there wasn't a man nor beast in that van that didn't have a hankering for some fresh catfish.

I will say in Dave's defense that he did allow as to how he didn't think it was a very good idea as I unlocked the back door, climbed the ladder on the back of his van, and then strode on top, the Monster Stick in hand. But after I started plucking four-foot catfish out of that truck with the regularity of a bran muffin with a fruit juice chaser and shoving them down through the driver's window to him, well, he hushed up.

I think everything would have gone just fine if I had cleaned out that first tank and let it go at that, but I decided I needed to take one cast into that second tank. Lying in that second tank, unbeknownst to me, in solitary confinement, sulking, was the biggest, baddest, meanest, one-eyed, tattooed, goateed, most unrehabitative catfish in the whole catfish farm system. That fish had nothing to lose, and he didn't care who he took out with him.

No sooner had he hit my hook then I knew what that bard, Bill Shakespeare from Stratford over on Avon Creek meant when he said, "Something in Denmark smells like a rub of Copenhagen." That fish started his run just as that truck started up a mountain at Flatwoods, and off we went like legislators to a free lunch.

There was that truck, putting out great clouds of diesel smoke and splashing catfish water all over the interstate. And there I was perched atop the van with my feet stuck underneath the luggage rack, a-fighting that fish with one hand and wiping splattered bugs off my glasses with the other. Dave was in the van with both hands on the wheel, dodging deer and trying to keep at least one tire on the pavement at all times while that fox pounced on those catfish like a chicken in a cricket barrel.

We were doing 170 miles an hour and figured to make Charleston in fifteen minutes. The fish was getting tired from all that uphill swimming he was doing, and things were looking pretty good until we rounded the curve coming off the mountain into Mink Shoals. You see, the catfish truck was in the right-hand lane, and me and Dave were in the left. Up ahead of us was a long stretch of empty highway. Empty, except for, about halfway down the road, straddling the center line, being operated by two little ol' blue-haired people who could have been Methuselah's grandparents, a motorhome the size of

Cleveland, and it was bearing a Buckeye license plate. Just like Cleveland, it was sprawling and rusty, hard to go around, and very dangerous to try and go through. So the truck veered right, and me and Dave veered left, and six miles of brand new fifty-pound carp cord caught the back of that motorhome and slingshot it nonstop to Tallahassee.

Dave, well, he done doughnuts down the median until he got us stopped. The truck careened on down the shoulder on the other side until he hit another truck parked down there, causing him to spill the last two thousand pounds of catfish right onto the interstate and shut it down for three hours. You might have seen that in the papers.

I believe it is fair to say that everyone involved in the whole mess was kinda upset. To start with, that truck driver, once he found out what happened, was as mad as any man who has just been slapped in the back of the head with four hundred wet catfish could be. The state trooper and the Department of Natural Resources officer who arrived on the scene, well, they got into a fight over jurisdiction. And the blue-haired people were mad because they had planned to drive the whole way to Florida at three miles an hour and didn't have any hotel reservations until October.

Well, Dave, he was mad because they slapped him with a DWI ticket. That's "driving with an idiot" for those who don't know. I thought that was pretty funny until they handed me my very own citation. You see, I wasn't driving, so they just slapped me with a BI, which stands for "being an idiot."

Personally, I don't think that part's very funny at all. I'm going to take them to court and I plan to fight them. That is, just as soon as I find me a law firm that don't hang up the phone every time I ask to speak to their best idiot lawyer.

SHIP OF STATE

The Monster Stick, my nine-foot, surf-casting rod with six miles of brand new fifty-pound Stren carp cord, and I took a short trip into the mountains a while back just to celebrate the season and waller in the beauty. I caught me a fine string of brook trout and fried them in a skillet with a mess of fresh dug ramps. I washed it all down with a mason jar of ice-cold Grandpa's spring tonic.

The birds were singing sweetly, and a warm breeze was blowing. I got sort of sleepy, so I nestled up in a big patch of mayflowers and rhododendrons, right between a junked school bus and a rusty old washing machine. I laid down beside the peaceful stream and took me a little nap. Well, folks, I don't know if it was the tonic or the ramps or maybe just the acid from that creek water, but I dreamed me a powerful dream. I dreamt I was the governor of the great state of West Virginia.

I dreamt that the whole state had turned into a mighty battleship, and I was at the bridge at the very tip top of Spruce Mountain. I could see everything that was going on. I'm here to tell you it was not a pretty sight. The good ship *West Virginia* was being besieged by a terrible storm. She was a-goin' down quick.

I dreamt the waves were crashing down on the ship. I dreamt half the crew were bailing out on me, and the rest were getting carted off to the brig. I dreamt that pirates were all around us and that every time one of those sneaky crewmen jumped ship, those pirates swooped in and dumped another carpetbagger right on my deck to take his place. I dreamt I saw great waves of unemployment and debt crashing onto the deck, sweeping all the teachers and doctors and laborers clean to North Carolina and beyond.

I don't know who it was that made me governor 'cause I can't imagine ever having enough money to buy my way into that office, but there I was, and I knew something had to be done. I stepped to the helm and grabbed the wheel with both hands, but the *West Virginia* would not respond. I looked back over my shoulder and saw why. The ship was hooked solidly to the rock bottom with an anchor of taxes so heavy it would sink the sun. The anchor was fastened to the ship by a crooked chain a mile long, a chain of lies and corruption and ignorance and blind following.

Well now, it made me mad to see my beautiful ship tied down like that. I don't know who sunk that chain down there, but judging by the rust and the seaweed and the barnacles, it had been hanging there for some time. It made me so mad that I scraped up a fire axe and headed to Charleston where that anchor was tied. I chopped loose the whole mess and let it fall to the bottom of the sea.

Well, wouldn't you know it, the *West Virginia* popped up just like cork, bands started playing bluegrass music, and I gathered all the passengers onto the deck. I passed out a mop, a bucket, some trash bags, and a couple of votes to each and every one of them. In no time, we had the *West Virginia* looking like "Almost Heaven" again.

We had the whole state shining real pretty, and everything was going just fine. Someone even climbed up to the top and finally finished putting the gold on the dome of the capitol. That's how busy we were. We sailed back into the fleet under a full head of steam and even had enough power to tow Louisiana and jump-start Arkansas on the way home. The whole way back, people were flagging us down and jumping back on board. We signed up Kathy Mattea as our cruise director, and she kept welcoming them back home to West Virginia. About the only trouble we had on that whole trip was when I got ready to park the state. I rammed the northern pan- handle into Pennsylvania so hard that it knocked Penn State plumb over to the Big Ten.

Well, I guess it was the bump that woke me up. Those ramps and that tonic were working on me something fierce. The honeymoon was over, and I wasn't the governor no more.

I have one thing to say about my term, and that's this: there's been a lot of governors before me who left the office with a headache and a bad taste in their mouths too, but darn few of them knew where they left the Ship of State parked.

BEWARE THE BABCOCK

George Webster Struthers, III, basically refused to acknowledge the twentieth century. Other than monofilament line and fiberglass fishing rods, there was little he thought the nineteen-hundreds had to offer. He just liked old things: old whiskey, old books, old banjos, and old trucks. His curly red hair and bushy, unruly mustache would have done Mark Twain proud. Webster wore suspenders, carried a pocket watch, and smoked Camel non-filter cigarettes. Hell, he even smelled musty.

Webster lacked but one thing that kept him from being a very fine old man: his age. He was twenty. Still, he was a good friend and fishing partner. What he did not possess in the wisdom acquired through longevity and experience, he made up. He just plain made up all sorts of astounding bits of fact and lore. He stuck by them too, with the obstinacy worthy of a man four times his age. If Webster decided that largemouth bass spent their larval stages beneath rotten logs on the forest floor, then Jacques Cousteau and the entire Calypso crew could not convince him otherwise.

Still, Webster managed very well not to be a know-it-all. A person he just met would likely be impressed with Web's wit and intellect but would not find him bullheaded or overbearing—usually. He was just fun to be around. He laughed a lot, loudly, and slapped his knees or the back of a friend in range. As a rule, he saved his infinite knowledge of the untrue for his closest pals, and that was when he was at his best. Webster, with a bottle of sour mash and an intimate audience, was a self-made genius of counterfeit facts.

Such was the occasion on a February evening in his father's basement. Dr. Struthers was a dentist and owned a fine home. Webster and I sat in plush, overstuffed easy chairs before a roaring fire, a jug of Tennessee sippin' whiskey between us. Scattered about us were various articles of fishing tackle laid out to receive some off-season maintenance. Cleaning and caring for gear is a poor substitute for fishing, but when the wind howls and the snow falls, it is better than nothing. It already had been a long winter, though, and by now we had done just about all the preparing and repairing of our equipment that could be done. At that moment, Webster was inspecting the springs of some red and white bobbers, and I was polishing sinkers. Finally, he could stand it no more.

Setting the bobbers aside, Webster picked up his drink, rose, and strode to the fire. He lit a smoke, tugged his suspenders, tossed back a snort, and cleared his throat. It was classic Websterese, and I knew I was about to receive a discourse. I glanced at the bottle, saw it was less than half full, and settled back in my chair, the benefactor of an impending oration.

I was not disappointed. He began with scathing comments on the softness of the modern American male, with footnotes on Perry and Amundson and the exploration of the poles. He threw in Lewis and

Clark and some scantily clad Indians wading through chest-high Rocky Mountain snow. Next came the Vikings, Laplanders, Eskimos, and Siberians. Barefoot cavemen slipped on glacial ice as they stalked woolly mammoths. Soldiers lay frozen to the ground in trenches on the Russian front.

His speech was passionate, eloquent. His hands knifed through the air, his arms cradled the earth. Ringlets of hair clung to his brow as his forehead dampened with sweat. Sparks flew from his pale blue eyes as he drew himself to his full height: five feet ten inches. Another foot and a stovepipe hat and he was Lincoln at Gettysburg. He spoke for nearly an hour as he narrated, again and again, man's triumph over bitter cold. It was awe-inspiring, and I groped for the proper response when he finished.

"You left out Santa Claus," I said reverently. "Besides, Webster, what in the heck are you trying to say?"

He was trying to tell me that we were going fishing. Tomorrow. Never mind the temperature was twenty degrees outside and bound to be colder around the mountain trout streams. I thought he was crazy. I told him so.

"Nonsense, son," he said. "Think of the men at Valley Forge."

I thought about them. It occurred to me that I had never heard about them catching trout and that the average soldier there lost three toes to frostbite. Webster was not dissuaded, though, and besides, my casting finger had been itching lately.

Blue Max, Web's faithful Ford, had served an honorable life. He was a testament to hard work, the epitome of a good West Virginia pick-up truck. His battered bed had hauled everything from Brownie troops on day trips to broken washing machines and empty beer cans bound for recycling. Of course, that was with former owners. Webster was against hard work and all it stood for. With him, Max had achieved a semi-retired state as a recreational vehicle. He still hauled beer cans, full and empty, but that was about it.

Max was no happier than I was to be leaving at seven A.M. the next morning. The truck bed squeaked and groaned as we loaded it, and I griped and moaned. It was really, really cold out. My only recourse was verbal abuse, but Max backed me up by refusing to start, a silent protest to this stupid trip. Our protests were futile. We were no match for Webster. He tortured Max into submission with jumper cables and bribed me with a breakfast beer. Max slipped into gear, and we were on our way to Babcock State Park in search of the elusive winter trout.

The road to Babcock, like the road to Heaven and most other roads in "Almost Heaven," is pitted with downfalls. I assume there are considerably fewer potholes on the road to Heaven, unless Gaston Caperton is governor there too. And I also figure there are a lot more beer and bait stores on the road to Babcock. We stopped several times to inspect the quality of service offered at these establishments and also took the road less taken, by accident, once or twice. We arrived at the campground in the late afternoon, which naturally was deserted. Webster could not believe our luck.

I suggested we use the remaining daylight to set up camp, but Web scoffed at the idea. "We have come to fish," he said, "and the tent can wait." As we hiked over the hill to Glade Creek, a light snow began to fall. By the time Webster decided it was dark enough for us to quit fishing, several inches blanketed the ground. We slipped and slid back up to Max.

Now, even for two Eagle Scouts like me and Web, pitching camp in the snow was no picnic. To further complicate matters, Webster, with his aversion to modern comforts, had neglected to pack a flashlight or lantern. He said that ol' Dan Boone never used 'em. I doubted if ol' Dan Boone ever had to unload a pickup in the dark or scrounge for firewood at a public campground. After a spirited argument culminating with Webster smashing his toes with a large rock that he was attempting to drive tent stakes into the frozen ground with, I won a minor skirmish. Although it was cheating, he allowed we could use the truck's headlights to assist us.

The earth never did yield to the tent stakes, so the tent was rigged with an elaborate web of ropes and strings anchored to most of the rocks and trees in the vicinity. Getting a fire going was even harder. All the consumable wood within three miles had been gathered long ago and burned by mom and pop and the kiddies for summer vacation hotdog roasts. What's more, we couldn't see. Unlike a flashlight, an F-100 truck is inconvenient to lug around the forest, and thus we had no light to aid the search. Eventually, as the night grew colder, and darker as Max's lights dimmed, I determined that our appendages and perhaps even our survival were at stake. On "Mr. Natural's" next foray into the woods, I resorted to desperate measures. It's amazing how quickly a remarkable blaze can be kindled from rotten tree stumps and useless tent pegs, especially if you use enough gasoline.

At long last, we were encamped. After a delicious meal of pan-fried trout (fish so fresh that, only hours before, they had been staring one-eyed through the plastic wrap at the South Charleston Kroger), Webster and I were ready to relax. We drank and smoked, hunkering by the fire, roasting our front-sides and innards while our butts froze. We sang rowdy songs and recounted past adventures until the wee hours of the night. At fifteen above, in a deserted campground in West Virginia, in February, the wee hours strike around 9 P.M. Somewhat drunkenly, we staggered to the tent, clumsily threading our way through the maze of guide wires and tent strings. With visions of early morning trout swimming in our heads, we crawled into our sleeping bags and drifted off to sleep.

I was awakened from a very unoutdoorsman-like dream of a heated waterbed and a remote control T.V. by a loud crash outside the tent. I had no idea what time it was, but peering out, I saw it was very dark. The crash woke Webster too. Dimly illuminated by the fire's dying embers, the campsite appeared empty. Despite our fears, no large bears or wild boars stood ready for the kill. Of course, in that situation, not knowing what's out there is more scary than knowing what is. With false courage, we poured out to investigate.

It turned out, much to our relief, that our intruder was only some type of small rodent that had knocked the skillet off the picnic table as it dined on the heads and bones of our trout. It had gone, leaving only its tiny tracks in the snow for us to argue over. I said they were raccoon tracks. Web decreed they were made by a weasel. He sternly pointed out to me, as if it were my fault, that a much larger beast might have just as easily snuck in with intentions of dining on our heads and bones. Fortunately, he explained, such an incident could be averted by a bright fire because such critters would not enter a camp so protected. We had a good bed of coals built up by now, so it was not nearly so difficult to entice our meager supply of wet wood to burn. I was relieved as the flames began to lick into those mushy logs, because it meant I would not have to try to convince Webster that Dan'l Boone would have considered burning state park picnic tables to save his camp from marauding animals.

After talking loudly about the guns and knives and other anti-invader equipment we had out of sight in the tent and strutting around with our chests stuck out, we returned to the warmth of our sleeping bags. I was asleep in an instant. I dreamed about a feather duster that tickled my nose. I brushed it away, but it returned. Then I woke with a start.

The feather duster was still there. Cautiously, I reached for my shoe in which my glasses lay safely tucked. Slowly, gently, I removed them from my shoe and pulled them into my sleeping bag to warm them up. I hissed at my slumbering pal.

"Webster," I whispered urgently, "wake up! There's something in the tent!"

If you've ever camped before, you'll realize that no words will wake up a tent mate faster. This time was no exception. I heard him suck in his breath. His back was to me; he dared not move until he knew what we were dealing with. I slid my glasses back up to my face. They were clear. I held my breath as my eyes adjusted to the dark and began to focus.

Meanwhile, back at the fire an old piece of knotty pine was coming to life. The fungus and rot that had encrusted it had dried, and its resinous heart was exposed. With a WHOOSH! of pent-up gasses, it erupted into a fiery blast of flame.

A marvelous chain reaction took place. The fire soared into a strategic tent rope. My vision cleared. I screamed "SKUNK!" The skunk skunked. The tent fell. The skunk fled.

This all occurred years ago. It is the type of incident that usually can be looked back upon with the passage of time and humorously recollected. That day has not yet come. I shall not forget breaking camp at 3 A.M. in the bitter cold with eyes that burned and watered from skunk juice. Even the tears that froze to our faces still don't seem funny. I'll long remember how Max, drained from flashlight duty, refused to start, requiring a four-mile hike to the ranger's house for a jump. Maybe the ranger, by now, chuckles when he remembers the two blue fishermen who cleared his sinuses that winter morn, but I doubt that too. He was not laughing then. Even George Webster Struthers, III, master of the optimum reconstruction of history for the greatest personal gain, has yet to release a version of this adventure that does not, in one way or another, leave us skunked at Babcock State Park.

SECTION 4

BIL

HELL'S CONGRESSMEN

I've had a hard time of late. You've heard of writer's block? Tennis elbow? Well, we liars get a little thing the doctors call *nocantellumlies*. In layman terms, it's called the Honesty Bug. I've been hit hard with it lately, and it's gotten to the point that I couldn't tell a lie if I cut down a cherry tree.

I know some people like to take a nice long walk when they need to clear their minds or concentrate. Other people like to put on their thinking caps, but I got a different way of doing things. When I get depressed or too honest, I like to put on my pink thinking ballet tutu and toe shoes, hop on my motor-scooter, drive around in the West Virginia twilight, and maybe stop in at a place of ill-repute for a few minutes. That usually makes for a good atmosphere and gets the creative juices flowing.

So there I was—this would have been about April some years back—tooling around on my scooter, when I noticed a place up ahead. It had a sign out front that read "Hell's Congressmen. Bar, Grill, and Hangout." Well, I'd heard of Hell's Angels and hell's bells, but I'd never heard of Hell's Congressmen, so I figured I'd wander in. As I got closer, I noticed there were motorcycles lined up in front as far as the eye could see, and they had all the perks your tax dollars could buy: drivers, wet bars, cell phones, the whole deal.

The building itself was a quaint little affair. It was set off the road a bit, had a long granite stairway leading up to twin, hand-crafted doors, and the place was divided into two wings with a sort of dome in the middle. I pushed open the door only to find the meanest, smelliest, nastiest, best-dressed bunch of fellas I'd ever seen. I sauntered up to the bar and ordered a tall, cool glass of milk. Well, I drink one milk, and it just leads to another, then another, and before long I'm taking strawberry Quik in that milk.

When I get that way, I start talking. I got to talking so much in that place I guess I was filibusting, and there's nothing a Hell's Congressman likes less than someone talking more than he does. The leader of that bunch came over to me and got right in my face. He looked at my pink thinking ballet tutu and toe shoes, then at my strawberry Quik. I was a vision in pink.

"Boy," he said, "what's your name?"

I said, "Bil, sir."

"Boy," he said, "let me see you do a pirouette."

I smiled shyly and said, "Oh, well, I don't actually dance ballet."

"Then how come you are wearing those clothes?"

"Well," I said, looking myself over, "you might not believe this, but it helps me think."

He didn't buy it. "Boy," he said, "let me see you do a plié."

"Like I said, sir, I don't dance ballet."

"Now, son," he was getting upset, "let me see you dance the Swan Lake."

"Look," I said, "with all due respect, I don't dance ballet. But I am glad you came over because now I finally have an answer to a question I've long pondered."

"What question is that?"

"Well, I've always wondered which was really uglier: actual congresspeople or those cardboard signs they leave by the roadside all year long."

That made him mad. That made the whole place mad. It suddenly got so quiet in there you could have heard a check bounce. The leader of that band started reaching into his jacket, and I figured he was going for a gun or a chain or a government sanction, but to my surprise, he pulled out a pair of toe shoes. Those other boys whipped out violas, clarinets, kettle drums, and the like. They busted into the *Nutcracker* quicker than you can say "Mikhail Baryshnikov."

From a critical standpoint, it was quite nice, though I must say the leader was being a bit of a prima donna. Usually I like to stay for this sort of thing, to get a little culture in my life, but I realized this might be my only chance for a getaway. I hit the door, hopped on my motor-scooter, and headed off into the night with my tutu fluttering in the wind. I had about a quarter-mile on those boys before they realized I was gone. When I looked back, they were pouring out the door of that place and jumping on their Harleys. The chase was on, and I gave them a ride, for sure!

I was on corridors A, B, C, D, E, F, G, and what there is of H before the night was through. And I was in Barbour, Braxton, Clay, Calhoun, Doddridge, Fayette, Gilmer, Hardy, Harrison, Monongalia, Taylor, Tyler, Tucker, Upshur, Wirt, Wetzel, Wayne, and Wyoming counties. Shoot, I reckon I was in every county there is trying to shake those boys, and before I knew it, I was lost.

Then, up ahead of me, I saw two parallel bars of

steel shining in the moonlight. I knew I wasn't lost no more. I could tell by the proud sheen on those bars that they could be nothing but railroad tracks, Weirton's world-famous steel fashioned into CS&X railroad tracks, at that. They stretched clear from Cowen to Grafton via Burnsville, Buckhannon, Carrolton, and Philippi, and folks, that's my home turf.

I still had a quarter-mile lead on those boys, and when I looked down the track, I saw a big light coming at me. Then I heard that low rumble and that deep whistle blow. The noise was shaking the rhododendron blooms and knocking cardinals out of their nests. I knew all that racket could be none other than six engines pulling a 168-car CS&X Monster Train loaded down with 19,364 tons of pure West Virginia bituminous coal. Talk about a getaway car!

I waited for the last coal car to come rolling by and jumped on. I was pulling my leg over the lip of that car when the first of the Hell's Congressmen caught up to me. He jumped up and grabbed my foot, the next guy grabbed his, and then the next guy grabbed his, and so on and so on, until I had the entire Hell's Congress flapping out behind that train like the tail on a kite.

By this time, I was starting to get a little tired. It's not easy to support Congress like that. They were starting to pull me off that train, but then I realized something. Suddenly I realized that I was better than all that, and I resolved right there that I wasn't about to be another Bil that Congress railroaded while they were dragging their feet! That's when I reached into my pocket and pulled out my seventy-four-function, stainless steel Swiss Army knife. It comes complete with a copy of the Constitution and the Bill of Rights, so I opened up those two documents and started waving them in the congressmen's faces.

They started cringing before those documents like Superman in front of kryptonite. They started dropping off that train, hitting the tracks, and getting up. Interestingly, all that law and all those falls must have had some effect on those boys because they started dusting themselves off and heading back to Washington. I believe they were suddenly hit by the Honesty Bug, and they were heading back to do some good. Now, I might have caused it all, but folks, I ain't here to brag. I'm just another American citizen trying to do his job. In fact, I'm nothing more than a lowly Bil up here on Capitol Hill.

Renegade Milker

I just cannot get enough rodeo, which is odd because I am not a cowboy and do not foresee myself becoming one. But as far as I'm concerned, nothing beats a rodeo for pure entertainment value. Take July three years ago down in Level Cross, North Carolina, for example.

Me, my wife, Paula, and our friends Chris and Brenda all bought tickets for a traveling bullride and buckin' bronco extravaganza. These little rodeos are a walking, talking, tobacco spit in the face of anti-By God Americans and all other non-patriots in general. They pass out Skoal to anyone who looks eighteen and sell greasy hamburgers so close to the cow pens that the animals certainly get the point: perform or else. It's the sort of thing that makes your average vegetarian self-righteous and the militant vegetarian mad enough to sue. I think that is why the burger salesmen still wear six-shooters.

When you sit down, you can watch all the stock milling around the arena until it gets dark, then somebody herds all the bulls off the field except the nastiest one they can find. He's usually a Brahman with long, well-sharpened horns and enough slobber and snot running down his snout to water the parched deserts of Arabia. Fireworks explode in the crisp night sky, and then a lone horseman rides into the ring. In one hand, he holds Old Glory; in the other, the Stars and Bars of General Lee. A microphone crackles, and you can hear the fuzz of a needle tracing across a worn LP. A voice says, "Please stand for the national anthem." A spotlight catches the rider, another the bull. And then comes the King's voice. Elvis sings out in the night, "Oh say can you see..." And then Elvis sings "Dixie." Unless you're farther south—then it's the other way around. If you get far enough south, there's no Old Glory at all.

Anyway, about twenty minutes into this particular show, the announcer started telling the crowd that any interested teams of three could pay fifteen dollars for the chance to milk a wild cow. The team that milks its cow first wins the pot. Well now, if that ain't an invitation to fun, nothing is. We four drew straws, and Chris, Brenda, and I each got to sign our very own waiver concerning broken bones, dismemberment, goring, and death.

Paula got out her camera and took a "before" picture of the three of us in clean clothes with our hair combed. As the bulb flashed, my mind produced an image of a newspaper spinning around, coming out of the black background like you see in the movies. When the paper quit spinning, there was the picture of the three of us smiling under the headline "Three Die in Tragic Milking Accident." Dying in a milking accident was just the sort of thing that really would make my mother mad.

Having never milked even the tamest of cows, I was interested in the best method for the task ahead of us. I asked a cowboy standing nearby. He smiled and said, "Simplest thing in the worl'. One 'a ya' grab 'er head and put 'er in a headlock, one grab 'er tail and lean way back on yer heels, and you, little lady, you grab them udders and milk away. Easier than ridin' a pound of groun' chuck." He hitched up his jeans, shot a stream of tobacco juice from his lips, and sauntered off. I had no idea if he was pulling our leg or giving us the straight dope, but it was all we had, and I figured it was better than bringing the cow roses and having Chris try to kiss her on the lips. (I must admit that I did not abandon the idea of Chris kissing the cow altogether.)

I've already stated that I am not a cowboy, so you might be able to understand why, in my mind's eye, the cow was about 150 pounds, lively but not easily agitated, and confined in one of the bull chutes. My mind's eye is a bit nearsighted, has a serious astigmatism, and is rather glaucomatic. My real eye found me staring down a fifty-foot rope tied around the neck of a three hundred-pound oppressed, radical feminist, "meat is murder," milk machine of a bovine who obviously was planning on turning me into fertilizer and was going to take great pleasure recounting the story in the barnyard later that evening. To make matters worse, I was wearing loafers, standing in eighteen inches of mud, and Chris was blowing the cow kisses. My only consolation was that six other teams of idiots were holding ropes as well.

Before the whole story comes out, let me backtrack just a little and explain the rules a bit more clearly. Seven cows each were contained in a separate chute with only their heads and necks sticking out. On the gate of each chute, a lazy-looking cowboy leaned his lanky body and told the cows detailed stories about the tortures inflicted by tenderfoot greenhorns trying to learn how to milk young cows. I believe I also heard the cowboy at my chute say, "Now the one in the loafers, he's gonna try and put you in a headlock.

You just duck yer head, and he'll go right under yer feet. Simple as that."

Anyway, when the starter gun sounded, the cowboys flung the gates open, and each team had to catch its cow. This meant trying to work your way up the rope to the cow's head while the cow moved away from you at maximum speed. Cows, mind you, are used to eighteen inches of mud and move much better in it than men in loafers. Once you caught the cow, you had to get the milk out of the udder and into a beer bottle, then take the bottle to a judge. You were not, under any circumstances, allowed to milk another team's cow.

So the gun sounded, and the cows charged out of the gates. Each cow ran away from the other end of its rope with such speed and abandon that suddenly there was a spiderweb-like tangle of ropes, each pulled as taut as a three hundred-pound cow could pull a rope, spinning around the center of the arena. Men paying attention only to their cow quickly were clotheslined and left moaning in the mud. My shoes are still where I left them, but even in sock feet, I was able to eat up that rope until I was about one cow's leg from our cow. Chris and Brenda were running flat out behind me, Brenda with the beer bottle clutched tightly in her hand. Paula was at the fence shouting encouragement and asking me where the key to the safety deposit box was, where I'd put the rainy-day cash, and if I could go ahead and toss her the car keys.

Now, you wouldn't think that a cow running at full speed could pick up its hind leg and kick like Chuck Norris, but I was learning a lot about cows. The hoof caught me in the gut and knocked me off my feet. My brain was too confused, or too mad, to tell my hands to drop the rope, so I slid face-first through the mud like a water-skier failing miserably at a stunt. Chris lunged over me and grabbed the cow's tail; I spun around on my butt and got to my feet. While the cow kicked at Chris, I worked my way toward her neck. My whole world had become a nightmare of wire-tight ropes, black hooves, blurry bovines, and the odor of fresh dung—mine and the cows'.

I could see the fence looming ahead as I got my arms around the cow's neck. My feet were essentially useless in the mud, so I picked them up and rested all my weight on the cow. She cornered like a racecar just inches in front of the steel fence, and my shoulder barely touched the metal post. Chris still was hanging tight to the tail when it whipped around and slammed him into the aluminum crosspieces like a flyswatter onto a table. The people on the other side stared wide-eyed, hoping Chris would explode like a NASCAR racer slamming into a wall. He didn't, but he did drop the tail. Brenda, however, had managed to grab the rope and now was digging her heels into the mud.

The cow was looking back at me as best as she could. I guess that's why she didn't see her sister standing broadside in front of us. I started to point but figured it would be best to keep both hands as near as I could to "inside the vehicle." A tremendous thud filled my ears when our Bessy leveled her sister. Brenda flew by on the rope. Chris, who had regained his feet and was running like a freight train to catch up, crashed into our cow's rear end. I dropped my feet into the mud and twisted them as deep as I could for footing. Chris grabbed the tail and leaned as far back as possible. The cowboy had not been lying to us; his plan was working, except that Brenda was nowhere to be seen.

The cow was winded, so as I pulled her head down

with my weight, she gave way a little until I was squatting in the mud and staring straight into the white of her eye. She seemed to be saying, "You just wait 'til I catch my breath. I'll show you mad cow!"

All around us, tan and black masses flew by, dragging muddy figures with no shoes and beer bottles. I was screaming for Brenda like a cowboy riding a cactus bareback on railroad tracks, when out of nowhere, a renegade milker appeared at my cow's udders and started milking her. I think our cow was starting to like me, or at least respect me, because that guy worked and worked that udder to no effect for some time. Chris and I were both too occupied, holding the cow in place and screaming for Brenda, to beat the guy up, so eventually a drop of milk landed in the bottom of his bottle, and he turned to go.

Well, hell hath no fury like two women scorned. Brenda returned to our cow just as the renegade milker turned to go. She still had the rope in one hand, and she deftly tied a loop around our milk thief's waist. She nodded at me and smiled. I looked to Chris, and we felt the first waves of laughter overcome us as we let go of our Bessy and slapped her on the hind end.

We were disqualified but rather satisfied.

Evil Ed,
The Early Engineer

I do not believe it is by any chance that the words "mourning" and "morning" sound exactly alike. The only time I like to see a sunrise is if I'm climbing into bed during it after a long night of adventure. As a rule, I like to sleep right through sunrises, allowing them to mature into a more reasonable hour. And as much as I love trains—hearing them thunder by, shaking the ground, and stirring up the dust—I must say I believe in moderation. When that fails, I believe in capital punishment.

Once upon a time an evil man was born, the sort of guy who likes to jog in the early morning mist. The kind of louse who appreciates birds chirping while the dew is still on the ground. That special breed of man who likes to be at the throttle of a 168-car monster train at 5 A.M., blowing the horn, taking curves too fast so that the tracks sing out in their horrid high pitch, causing dogs to go mad and children to awake screaming. His name was Evil Ed, the Early Engineer.

Now, this all occurred when I was still in college, living in McCuskey Dorm in a room that faced the tracks. Evil Ed drove the morning train and took a sadistic pleasure in coming by our dorm on Saturday and Sunday mornings. He'd start blowing his horn in short blasts almost a mile off, to wake us, and then lay it on full bore as he rolled past the dorm. Some mornings, when he was ahead of schedule, he'd stop the train right outside our rooms and blow until bottles sallied out of all the windows of our building, exploding all along the train.

Enough was enough. We decided to put our partially educated minds together and come up with a solution. One student suggested a giant ramp: "We'll just launch him into space." Another idea was to dig a huge hole in the tracks, cover it with branches and sod to camouflage it, and let Evil Ed fall, "just like trappin' an elephant." One more student suggested we steal the tank in front of the armory and blast Evil Ed. A Liberal screamed, "Fascist!" This was met by the idea that the hippies could have a sit-in on the tracks, at which point somebody called the ACLU. It quickly became evident that, if the situation were to be corrected, the responsibility once again would fall to Paul, Steven, and myself.

We brewed and brooded over the problem for long hours, even skipping class when necessary. We thought up scheme after scheme, and although the tank idea was never far from our minds, we resolved that the train should be spared at all costs. We didn't sleep. We stood by the tracks in the wind and rain. We had clipboards, calculators, and slide rules. We calibrated, analyzed, weighed, measured, and figured until we knew everything there was to know about Evil Ed The Early Engineer and his train. As we suspected, he was not a native West Virginian.

Once we knew Evil Ed's style, we learned the lay of the land. We photographed the curves, the bridges, the tunnels. We graded the slopes of the hills, determined times 'twixt various points A and E, diagrammed, reckoned, and then went over it all again. It was a trying time, but we endured.

For the most part my companions and I, along with the rest of the student body of West Virginia Wesleyan College, were known for our superior mental capabilities, our attendance, and our general seriousness about studies. Seldom a semester went by when perfect attendance wasn't recorded campuswide. The Bell Curve arched somewhere between A and A+ at Wesleyan, but as this train ordeal progressed, the strain began to show. It weighed on all of us, taxing our minds to the hilt and eating away at our nerves. As the stress built, the student body came together. Fundraisers were organized, banners were created, and posters hung. The frats made t-shirts, the sororities hugged. It became a movement. Classes were suspended, the library closed, only the cafeteria remained open.

Being the modest types that we are, Paul, Steven, and myself accepted the role of leadership with humility. We attended the banquets with a blush, made a minimum of speeches, and declined to go on national television. We did, however, accept the donation of a local building with gratitude. It became our map room.

We built a huge scale model of the tracks, leaving nothing out. We started in Cowen and laid track all the way to Grafton, including Burnsville, Buckhannon, Carrolton, and Philippi along the way. We took special care to make the mountains as beautiful as we could; we made the rivers blue and even tossed in a satellite dish, a few rusted appliances, and an old car, just for credibility's sake. It was a wonderful model but useless until we had a plan to plan. And then Paul had his dream. We tried the idea out, honed it to perfection, kicked ourselves for not thinking of it earlier, learned our parts, and then moved down to the tracks.

The sun was still under the horizon, and the mountain air had a chill to it. The mist was rising off the Buckhannon River, and an old owl was hooting. It was pleasant, but I hoped it would be the last morning I would see for a long time to come. We yawned, stretched, divided the student body into work teams, and got down to business. Each group worked quickly, laying its section of the trap, and then we all gathered behind the dorm to watch.

In the distance we heard Evil Ed throttle up and blast his horn. The whole student body crossed their fingers. Evil Ed came round the bend; everyone held their breath. Evil Ed's eyes flared with devilish joy when he saw he had an audience, and his eyes glowed as he reached for the brake. He was going to slow down, savor the moment, watch our faces as he made his racket going by. But as he worked the brake, his glare wilted into dumb confusion. No screech came from the wheels, and his mouth dropped as the train gained speed rather than slowing. He was on the last slope before town, and the lard-coated tracks just slid Evil Ed right by us all. Part One of the plan came off without a hitch. Jeers and hand gestures met Evil Ed's cries for help.

Part Two was a little hairier. Steven had to run along the narrow boards of a platform we had built beside the tracks and then leap onto the coal cars. We silently watched him jump. He landed soft as a cat, then carefully made his way to the junction between the engine and the 168 coal cars loaded with 19,364 tons of pure West Virginia bituminous coal. Steven slipped the pin out of the coupling unit, and the cars rolled to a stop. The engine, however, now liberated from its burden and with Evil Ed applying the throttle, shot down the track at an unprecedented speed.

And then the climax, the finale, the ripe tomato, Part Three. I only wish I could have seen the look on Evil Ed's face as the tunnel came into view (though I can't say that I'd have wanted to wash his underwear). The tunnel team had sealed the entrance with a wall of toilet paper painted to look like rubble. I can only assume that Evil Ed fell against the back wall of the engine, arms crossed over his head, as he tore through the paper. Perhaps he sighed with relief, happy to be alive after that, but his joy would have lasted only until he saw the other train in the tunnel, headed his way. With the lard still thick on the tracks, he must have crashed into the oncoming train full speed ahead, only then discovering it was just a mirror. Rumor has it his scream still can be heard echoing off the walls of that tunnel.

Our plan came off without a hitch. Nary a car on the train was damaged, and the engine hadn't even sustained a scratch. And Evil Ed, well, he still drives the trains past our dorm, but he never goes too fast, never blows the horn, and never comes before the sun is well over the mountain tops.

My First Deer Camp, a Plastic Sleeping Bag, and a Full Bladder

always have been a fan of the Great Outdoors. I am an Eagle Scout, a backwoods adventurer, and otherwise the kind of guy whose mother and wife continually kick out of the house. However, as a child I never could talk my mother into getting me a gun. I'd get Dad all wired up to go out and buy me a lever-action Winchester .30-30 for Christmas, but then Mom would step in and throw down the kibosh on the whole deal. Dad and I both would sulk. The long and the short of it is that I never got to do any hunting as I was coming up, and so I never really caught "buck fever." But then a wonderful thing happened. I met a girl whose father was a tank commander, a forest ranger, and a proponent of guns. I married her right away. One Christmas later, I had my .30-30.

After I finally joined the ranks of the American Gun Nuts (who are not to be confused with the more dangerous Armed American Nuts), I met a guy who promised to take me hunting, and I bugged him until he made good. Twenty-seven years of reading hunting magazines and Jack London stories goes a long way to build expectations in a guy's head, but I have to say that my friend's hunting camp was a sight to behold and an answer to all my dreams. I sort of guessed that if I arrived late enough, all the work of setting up camp would be done, and I could just settle into my bag with a stogie and a cup of bad coffee. I was right.

The camp was picturesque: a walled canvas tent with the chimney of a woodstove protruding from the rear, fine white smoke disappearing into the dusk. The tall grass was leaning in the wind, and the mountains of West Virginia rose into the sky. A hunter in a plaid jacket was chopping firewood as another lit his pipe and studied a relief map. They were discussing the merits of their pre-1964 rifles, complimenting each other on last year's kills, and begging to be allowed to cook breakfast.

It was a truly spectacular site, only the tent was really a pop-up camper that bore the word "Apache" in rusted chrome letters along the side. (It's no wonder the Native Americans dislike the way we've used their names. No self-respecting Apache would have ever hauled anything like that camper behind his horse.) The camper was mostly plastic, except for the holes, and was the only item in the camp that actually was pre-'64. The woodstove was two propane burners working overtime, and the field was a wide spot on a muddy road. The wind and mountains are authentically represented, but the sum total of the hunters' conversation that would be both interesting and decent enough to reprint might run something like this:

"   ."

The work having been completed, and the cold being furious, we settled into our sleeping bags and rested up for the morrow's hunt. I would like to say that I got a good night's sleep, but the fact is I should have "emptied out" before I settled in.

Most people are familiar with the term "empty out," but for those of you who are not, I will explain. When I was a child, I was highly skilled at bed-wetting. I could wet the bed two, three times a night without even waking. My parents resorted to a rubber sheet to protect the mattress, and thus I often had dreams that I was up and urinating and that I was drowning. Often I awoke to discover I was actively engaged in both activities. So my dad, every night before I got into bed, would say, "Did you empty out?" I would trot to the bathroom, empty out, and hit the hay. Hours later, Dad would come in, get me up, and then hold me over the potty until I emptied out again. Once, he begged and begged as he held me over the bowl in the middle of the night only to look down and realize he was holding my Snoopy doll instead of me. But that's another story all together.

Anyway, here I was in my sleeping bag, the wind howling, the camper freezing, and me in my union suit having not emptied out.

As long as I'm this far off the subject, my sleeping bag is a German Army surplus item that is completely waterproof due to the fact that a heavy plastic rain poncho zips over it. I picked it up in-country when I was acting as a special attaché representing American high school students. The picture certainly must be coming into focus for you by now: me, a proficient bed-wetter, not emptied out and zipped into a poncho in a pop-up camper on my first hunting trip ever. I couldn't risk getting up lest I froze, but I couldn't risk falling asleep lest I inadvertently fill my German Army zip-lock bag with processed coffee and then suffer the ultimate humiliation by being frozen into a yellow snow popsicle.

Well, in the end I got up, but I had struggled so deep into the night that I didn't get enough sleep, and as a result, I didn't wake up until after sunrise. Apparently my fellow hunters were all bed-wetters as well because they all were still sound asleep when I woke up. Solidarity is one of the nicest things about hunting camp.

My comrades assured me that the breakfast we had was traditional hunting camp food. Having done my fair share of camping, I was skeptical, but traditions are traditions, and so I ate my frozen chocolate custard pie like everyone else. I could hear the deer for miles around whispering, "Chocolate custard pie? They could eat that at home. They don't have to shoot at us for an excuse to eat frozen custard pie for breakfast." As fate would have it, they were right. I ate the pie, Tom ate the pie, and Frank ate the pie. Not one of us shot a deer. Scott ate the pie too, but he was more fortunate. That is to say, there is one less smart-aleck deer in the world thanks to Scott.

Eventually we did manage to actually hunt, and as a novice in new territory, I became Scott's apprentice. He led me up the path, told me to shut up, sat me down at the edge of a field, and told me to watch both the woods and the field. He vaguely described the other side of the rise I was facing, pointed, said "I'll be over there," and tromped off.

To this day, I believe he had been making payments to the Deer Fairy as regularly as my grandmother pays the Christmas Club. Either that or there was a dead deer sale on the other side of that mountain and Scott had a coupon and a couple of dollars. Scott's head disappeared below the rise, there was a gunshot, and then he was lugging the carcass of a nice five-point back over the hill. He swears he gave me the best spot, but he still won't let me top that rise.

We didn't see another deer the whole trip. I have to say, though, I was not too sad. I guess I just never contracted "buck fever," but after we hiked through five miles of underbrush in seven layers of clothes, I was not overly eager to shoot a deer because I was not overly eager to drag it back. Besides, we had more frozen pie back at the camper.

Subjectibility
of the Word "Stupid"

If you measure my parents' canoe, you will discover that it is eighteen feet from bow to stern, but you better have a flexible ruler because it's shaped like a roadkill armadillo. And wear leather gloves because it's a twisted wreck of aluminum waiting to give you tetanus—to hear my parents tell it anyway.

Like all great disasters, the ordeal started out innocently enough. My parents had to go to Canada for a week, and I had to stay home. I was a pretty good kid and generally stayed out of trouble. Besides, my dad had given me the same useful advice he always gives me just before he leaves me alone with his valuable stuff, like the car, the house, and the canoe. He said, "Don't do anything stupid!" I had taken the advice to heart. The breakdown occurred in the subjectibility inherent in the word "stupid."

You see, it was spring, the rains had just quit, and the rivers were a fury of white water and leaping fish. Everything was perfect, in my mind, for canoeing, but not so in Dad's mind. To Dad it would have been stupid to take the canoe out in such raging waters. As far as I could see, it would have been stupid not to.

Call it rebellion, call it generation breakdown, call it whatever you like, but my folks no sooner had pulled out of the drive, waved goodbye, and made the corner then I had the canoe lashed to the top of my car, my dog in the back seat, and my fishing gear in the trunk. I drove up to the covered bridge in Carrolton and stood on the bank of the Buckhannon River, just watching for a few minutes. The water definitely was up. In fact, that covered bridge spans the Buckhannon River at its narrowest point, so the water was moving through the high banks like it was coming out of a firehose. It was a continuous blast of foam moving at near light speed. I untied the canoe, loaded the fishing gear, and pulled the dog out of the car.

My dog, Buck, the half-shepherd, half-basset super-dog who knows no fear and takes to water like a porpoise, seemed a little uneasy. It was the first time I'd ever seen him nervous around water, but I just figured there was a rattlesnake or a copperhead nearby making him jumpy. When he would not step into the canoe on his own, I lifted him in. He ran to the bow and curled up on a life jacket, biting through the straps so that it was securely locked in his mouth. I got behind the canoe and gave it a push.

I had never before seen a canoe accelerate like that one did. The front end vanished into the foam, and I had to jump into the stern like a tardy bobsledder. Somewhere, eighteen feet in front of me, I could hear my dog wailing, but I could not see a thing. The roar was deafening, and we seemed to be in a vortex of logs, diapers, and water moving so fast that the friction between individual molecules caused little fires to flare up.

We seemed to be moving straight and at a fair clip,

so I put my paddle down and baited my hook. I had just cast when we arrived at the place where the banks drop off suddenly and the river widens to twice the size it is when it passes under the bridge. We virtually exploded out of the wall of water we had been riding in, and I suddenly understood what the wadding in a shotgun must feel like as it blasts free of the barrel. Smaller objects, such as sticks and rocks, blew way out in front of me, but the canoe was so heavy that we only flew a few short feet before descending back toward the water.

Being that I was the heaviest object in the canoe and sitting in the stern, the lighter front end started to rise. I put my fishing pole in my mouth and grabbed hold of the gunwales with both hands. It looked as though the landing was going to be rough. The blasting wind had all but folded my eyelids under my brow, so I had no choice but to watch the events unfold. I could see my dog, holding fast to his life jacket, still curled up in the front end.

He was looking at me as though he now understood what my father meant by "stupid." The stern of the canoe dropped into the water like a saw blade into a pine board. A sheet of water twelve feet tall rooster-tailed behind us, and steam rolled out from beneath the canoe.

I looked over to the shore and was surprised to see three kayakers standing on the bank. They were decked out in colorful wetsuits and waving at me while hastily grabbing the emergency throw-ropes clasped to their belts. I could not help but wonder why they looked so horrified and why they were reaching for their rescue gear with such vigor. I shrugged my shoulders, figuring they were just out practicing water rescue techniques, and then I looked back toward the river.

Remember the asteroid belt Han Solo pilots the Millennium Falcon through in *The Empire Strikes Back?* Well, I, my dog, and that aluminum canoe were headed toward its earthly cousin at approximately the same speed the Falcon would have been making— only my Chewbacca was a half-breed basset hound, and my ray-gun was a cracked wooden paddle.

The bow of the canoe was beginning to drop toward the surface of the river like the nose of a landing supersonic jet, and the steam plumes were ebbing. I was just starting to develop a plan when I noticed Buck was crouched on the front deck plate like the hood ornament on a Jaguar. He still had his life jacket locked in his teeth when he sprang from the craft and landed in a shallow pool. He leapt from the bow with such force that the front end submerged violently, causing the stern to shoot straight up. If you've never seen a canoe suddenly stand up in the midst of a raging river, I recommend it, provided you are standing at a safe distance. If you've never been in a canoe cartwheeling downstream, well, after about the third rotation, all the novelty goes out of the situation.

The canoe did not slow until a prehistoric pillar of limestone, which had survived countless assaults by rain, ice, logs, and fire in its billion years of existence, survived yet another catastrophic collision. The canoe bent around that stone like a twist-tie on a bread wrapper. As coincidence would have it, the kayakers still were practicing their lifesaving skills and had happened to toss their throw-ropes within arm's reach. I grabbed hold, and they pulled me to the bank. Buck would not come near me.

It was three days before the water dropped low enough for me to be able to haul the canoe out of the stream. I took it home and right away went to work repairing it. I'm pretty handy, after all, with a hammer and a crowbar. When I had the canoe looking modestly straight, I called my parents in Canada and explained the barest details of the events. I figured the remaining day of their visit and the thirteen-hour drive home would give them plenty of time to focus their thoughts on other matters, perhaps even forget the whole affair altogether. I figured they at least would have come to the conclusion that they had overreacted on the phone and would just be happy that I, their baby, was unhurt.

Maybe I should have called sooner. They had not forgotten, and they were very critical of the post-crash body work that I had so lovingly perpetrated on the canoe. I was amazed by how well they remembered its original shape and how unwilling they were to accept my carefully rehearsed ploy of "What? No. It's always been bent there." At that point I shrugged my shoulders and said, "Factory defect, I suppose." Furthermore, I believe they were a bit disappointed that I was not in any way broken, bruised, or lacerated. It has long been my rule that if it didn't hurt, I'd do it again—especially if I didn't own the equipment. Is that so stupid?

I'M SCARED OF FISH

My brother is the fisherman in the family. I tend to let that stand as his calling, and I rarely interfere. It's not that I do not like fishing; I find it as relaxing as the next guy, and I even do it now and again. It's just that I don't like to catch fish. The truth is I'm a bit frightened by the deep. But I contend with the utmost conviction that I am not a chicken just because I am scared of fish. I can tell you, for example, that my cousin and I, on a dare, walked twenty-six miles in the bear-infested woods of northeastern New Mexico wearing nothing but loincloths, armed only with black powder rifles, and carrying nothing but bloody raw liver in necessary bags. It took courage. It does not prove I am not an idiot, but here I'm only trying to prove I'm not a chicken. My idiocy is a whole other work.

Speaking of raw liver, when I do fish, I fish for catfish, but I keep the liver way up on shore. If any fish is man enough to come out of the water after my bait, I want it to be plumb tuckered-out by the time it gets to me. I also try and use only the freshest liver available. I look at the dates on each package in the grocery store before I buy. I figure the oldest catfish will bite only on the rankest bait, so by my figuring,

I'll catch catfish, but only small, young, dumb ones who'll bite on anything. When my fear is at its worst, I fish with rosebuds.

In all honesty, I really am quite scared of fish. I don't like to be out in the ocean because I always assume that a multi-tentacled, venomous-finned, razor-toothed leviathan is sizing me up from beneath. There I would be, the lunch of some creature that Jules Verne and Gary Larson collaborated on, and people would not know whether to laugh or scream as I was swallowed up.

River fish frighten me as well—you never know if the fish on the end of your line has just eaten the carcass of a bovine that died of mad cow disease.

Despite my fears, I love to fish. I am probably the only person you'll ever meet who thinks bravery is achieved by landing a bream, but I get out there and do it. I prefer, however, to fish in clear lakes and rivers so I can see what's coming at me before it breaks the surface. And I only buy cheap gear because if I have to abandon my pole, I don't want to be out too much money. If I can help it, I only fish in small ponds. I figure if the pond is only twenty feet across and four feet deep, and I don't see the tail or fins of anything sticking out, well, I'll probably be pretty safe. I've even considered stocking my bathtub.

But again, I love to fish. I like the shock that runs through my body when I feel a hit, when the pole bends over, and the line starts running out. In all truth, I get more out of the hit than most people. Most fishermen just get the shock of excitement, the feeling of accomplishment. I get the thrill of knowing that I might die. I think I probably get the same feeling big game hunters get when their rifles misfire or they only wound the charging elephant. For me, hooking a fish, even a small fish, is the start of mortal combat.

I even try to avoid fishing with minnows. I don't mind hooking up a cricket or a worm, but reaching into a bucket of minnows that just might have inherited the genes of a piranha? That's just insane.

I cannot say where these fears developed or why my psychological makeup is so illogical when it comes to fishing, but I can say that, as a result of my phobias, most people don't like to go fishing with me. I'll be the first to admit that a peaceful lakeside outing ruined by a blood-curdling scream and a grown man sobbing over a six-inch bass, saying "It was huge! It was this big!" while holding his thumb and forefinger as far apart as possible is sort of sickening, so I go alone.

I go alone for other reasons, too. If you take experienced fishermen with you on an outing, they're bound to watch you go through all the motions of readying your pole and tying on your hook. Old fishermen love to tell young guys about this or that knot, and some even grab your stuff and tie one on for you. I appreciate such chivalry, but I have developed my own knots. I try to tie them in secret—in the dark if possible. I justify the whole process by saying that I like the fish to have a fighting chance. Let's face it, if you tie a good enough knot, there's no way a fish will break it. I don't tie a good enough knot, and the old pros hate it.

My hooks are not standard hooks, either. What I try to do is find a curved stick with some bark hanging loose. I then try to barely catch the bark on my line. If a fish bites the stick and stays on, well that's that. But if the hook somehow, miraculously, slips off, well, then it's biodegradable and no one will step on it and get tetanus. What's more, I won't inadvertently poke a fish on his way home from a stressful day at work, thereby sending him into a rage such as has never been witnessed. Like I say, the old guys don't like me along.

So what's my point? Well, I don't really have one. I guess I just wanted to let everyone know that I'm scared of fish. Maybe it's bigger than just me. Maybe there are a million latent fishaphobics out there who cringe every time they open their mailboxes and a largemouth bass is leaping at them from the cover of an outdoors magazine. Maybe we could form a support group. Maybe we could form a movement with a political agenda and a bunch of lobbyists. Maybe I won't have to write a whole 'nother story just to prove my idiocy. Maybe this one will kill that bird as well.

A Comment on
My Brother's Death

My brother Paul died in January 1998. He did not invent the West Virginia State Liars Contest; for that we honor Ken Sullivan, but Paul essentially put the contest on the map. Paul won the contest six times, often knocking my best efforts into second or third place. But losing to Paul was like having Babe Ruth beat you in a home run contest: it just made sense. He was the master, and he did the storytelling world a favor by upping the standard between a good story and a great story.

This is roughly the text of the eulogy I delivered at Paul's funeral. Mind you, I am a Methodist minister in the West Virginia Conference, and both the most recent former bishop and the current bishop were present.

———

I only have one problem with the Bible. There aren't enough jokes. Can you honestly tell me that Jesus, the Son of God, didn't spin a yarn every now and then? I mean, come on, the guy hung out with fishermen. Fishermen are almost by definition the crudest people on the face of the earth. They are a cross between sailors and rednecks. That alone stands as proof of God's sense of humor. Jesus and the disciples must have cut-up around the campfire at night. We know that God loved fishermen; surely God loves a good joke, too.

My brother's favorite author was Mark Twain. Paul revered Mark Twain. Now, in the Lepp family, "revere" is a strong word. We are a family that has no problem comparing ourselves to great historical figures and saying, "Well, that Bach was pretty good, but listen to this..." So to say that Paul held Twain above himself is saying something. But anyway, Mark Twain once said, " I like a good story, well told. That is the reason I am sometimes forced to tell them myself." My brother Paul took that statement to heart. Paul loved a good story, well told. There are many storytellers he enjoyed listening to, but in the end, he was compelled to create his own tales and present them his way. Thank God he did.

God gave my brother the gift of story so that he could amuse and entertain us all. And then God gave us all a sign as to how much God loves a good story, well told, by making my brother a fisherman. God loves fishermen. I have no doubt that God loves my brother.

—Bil Lepp

Notes on the Stories

Flying High: This story, Paul's first entry into the Liars Contest, is based on an actual plane crash that happened at the Charleston airport in the early Eighties. A plane full of marijuana indeed did roll off the end of the runway, but whether or not Paul had anything to do with it, well, you've read the story. Creating a story out of the headlines was a trend that Paul would often employ in his storywriting. He followed West Virginia news carefully and turned ordinary stories into extraordinary events. This story won Paul his first "West Virginia's Biggest Liar" title. Paul told this story a thousand times at events all over West Virginia and the East Coast. It was published in *Goldenseal* magazine in the Spring '87 issue.

There Stands A Bridge: When Paul didn't find a good story in the news, he often relied on his other sure-fire tactic: pick something unmistakably West Virginian and run with it. The New River Gorge Bridge is one of West Virginia's most famous landmarks, and Paul was always interested in promoting West Virginia. So he created this story. If "Flying High" introduced Paul, this story started his legacy. For the second year in a row, he won the Liars Contest. He went on *Mountain Stage* and *Michael Feldman's What Do You Know?* with this story. It was published in the Spring '88 *Goldenseal*. I think this was Paul's favorite story.

Three Wishes: Having introduced the Monster Stick, Paul now goes back and explains the origins of his famous fishing pole. This story was not used at the Liars Contest but rather was written to explain the myth. Paul was a great fan of J.R.R. Tolkien, C.S. Lewis, and all the Round Table business. This story reflects those influences, but it also plays on the sort of bumbling superhero who turns up in so many traditional stories.

Unnatural Disaster: Paul was back at the news. This story has its origins in the wreck of the Valdez up in Alaska, but again Paul West Virginia-ized it. It would lead to his third Biggest Liar title. This story was published in the Spring '90 *Goldenseal*.

Weather or Not: Again, Paul relied on his "all things West Virginia" plan for the contest. Knowing that the judges and the crowd would be composed mostly of natives, Paul looked to please them all. He again picked a West Virginia landmark, Sutton Lake, and then proceeded to name half the towns in West Virginia. This was his third try at the Liars Contest, and he already was setting a new precedent. The contest started out just promoting storytelling in general, but Paul was making sure that the West Virginia in the title was adhered to. Largely because of Paul, entries from this point on included serious nods toward our home state. Although Paul was forging new paths, he was not untouchable, and this story took second place in the '88 contest. It was published in the Spring '89 *Goldenseal*.

Buck Ain't No Ordinary Dog: This story stands as a landmark in my personal storytelling career. It was my 1996 shot at the Liars Contest title, and although it was not the first time I won the contest, it was the first time

I beat Paul. He had leveled my best attempts in years past, but he could not beat Buck-Dog. Buck is an honest-to-God dog whose parents really were basset and shepherd. This is his first appearance in my stories but certainly not the last. If you ever saw him, you would understand why he became the topic of my stories. He looks exactly like I describe him in the story. This tale was printed in the Spring '97 *Goldenseal* and published in the *Fayette Tribune*.

Buck Versus the Government: This is the second of the Buck-Dog stories presented at the Liars Contest. Buck is further adorned with superpowers and even takes on politics and militiamen. Buck once again helped me to a first place win, this time in 1997. Not only was this story featured in the Spring '98 *Goldenseal*, but Buck and I were pictured on the cover.

Jonah: The Real Story: This was the third story of mine at the Liars Contest to be bested by my brother. He beat me with his 1995 "No Stranger to Trouble." I wrote this tale during my first year at Duke Divinity School. I was learning an awful lot of technical biblical study techniques, and this tale was the end result. It might be a little irreverent, but I still think it gets the message of the story across. I can't decide if I should have been more, or less, reverent to win first place. This story appeared in the Spring '96 *Goldenseal*.

With God as My Witness: Paula and I were drifting off to sleep in a train car speeding across Slovakia. Shelley and Eric and Chris and Brenda were playing euchre and I heard Eric say, "Man, I dig all these Jacks!" In my half-slumber I heard it as "Man, there's pigs on these tracks!" That set my mind drifting back in time to my college dorm, and there was Drake, splattered in pink paint and saying, "Well, what do ya think of my submarine now?" Next thing I knew he was talking about putting the thing on wheels and rolling it down the abandoned tracks.

The Seventh Second: This is my baby. This is the first story I wrote for the Liars Contest, and it gave a good showing, placing second to "Ship of State." It introduces all my favorite topics except Buck, including my Swiss army knife and CS&X trains. I was sure this story would win the contest and that the Victronx and CS&X would be knocking down my door to endorse me. It's been nine years...

The style of this tale clearly is influenced by my sitting around many contests listening to Paul work his magic. This story appeared in the Spring '91 *Goldenseal.*

Carp in the Garden of Eden: This is one of the first stories Paul ever wrote in that tall tale vein. He wrote it in the early '80s after, I strongly suspect, reading the collected short stories of Mark Twain. It also was the first story of his that I ever read. I was pretty young and rather certain he would go to Hell for writing it, as would I for reading it. I'm fairly sure that the memory of this story influenced my "Jonah" story. Dad even preached part of "Carp in Eden" one Sunday morning.

The Carpman's Creed: It is only by special permission from the Brotherhood of the Fin that this creed is allowed to be reproduced. Please respect it.

Walleyed Suckers and Waterdogs: Paul was almost ten years older than I and did a lot of things before I was out of training pants. This is one of those adventures. So many of our stories are based in truth that I can only assume that this one is at least partially true. I know Rebus Ward was Paul's good friend; I know they went fishing in Virginia; I know why somebody would call Paul "Possumhead." I think this story is merely a toned down account of actual events.

Lightning Bugged: This was not a lie Paul entered into the contest but a story that falls instead into the "Waterdogs" category. You can see, however, that it is more embellished than some stories but less fantastic than the lies presented on stage. I would not be surprised if this story were a rough draft for the Liars Contest.

No Stranger to Trouble: This story beat Jonah. This was at least the seventh story Paul brought to the Liars Contest, and it has all his usual elements. A truckfull of catfish really did crash on the highway a few weeks before the contest, and Paul just wove it all in, natural as day. The prune juice and old folks are classic gems of Paul's creative genius. This story appeared in the Spring '96 *Goldenseal.*

Ship of State: While generally presenting an air of aloofness toward politics, Paul was actually a close follower of it all. He had well thought-out gripes against the corruption and fumblings sometimes committed by West Virginia government. He used his talent as a storyteller to present satire. This tale won the '90 contest and was the first of a number of politically motivated stories. The '90 contest was the first year I entered, and thus this is the first of Paul's stories that outshined mine. It was printed in the Spring '91 *Goldenseal.*

Beware the Babcock: Like "Walleyed Suckers..." I honestly believe this story is a slightly altered autobiographical account, or at least firsthand account, of events that really took place in Paul's life.

Hell's Congressmen: This story was written during the 1992 presidential campaign. It was the first time I ever won the Liars Contest; Paul stayed out of it that year. This story was published in the Spring '93 *Goldenseal.*

Renegade Milker: Except for the part about Brenda tying the Renegade Milker to the cow, this story is true. I swear. If I'd made it up, we would have won the money.

Evil Ed, the Early Engineer: These are all first-run lies that either were scrapped or rewritten into totally different stories. Of course, scrapping a story does not mean that it is not a good story, just not right for the big show. "Evil Ed," in all honesty, somehow morphed into the "Jonah" story after months of rewrites.

My First Deer Camp, a Plastic Sleeping Bag, and a Full Bladder: I am ashamed at how true this story is. I think I wrote it in an attempt to free my psyche from the devastating truth of the matter. I am a better man for it.

Subjectibility of the Word "Stupid": I will admit to a little bending of the facts and even some conflation here. I did wreck my parents' canoe, and they were in Canada at the time, and I did get saved by a band of experienced kayakers who explained that they had abandoned the river due to the extreme high water. I added Buck to the story for fun. He would not have been amused.

I'm Scared of Fish: This story is pure nonfiction. In fact, it is because of things like waterdogs that I am scared of fishing. I do fish quite a bit, but I normally left the task to Paul. He had the stomach for it.

—*Bil Lepp*

Notes on Publications

The following stories were published in *Goldenseal* magazine: "Flying High," Spring 1987. "There Stands a Bridge," Spring 1988. "Weather or Not," Spring 1989. "Unnatural Disaster," Spring 1990. "Ship of State" and "The Seventh Second," Spring 1991. "Hell's Congressmen," Spring 1993. "No Stranger to Trouble" and "Jonah: The Real Story," Spring 1996. "Buck Ain't No Ordinary Dog," Spring 1997. "Buck Versus the Government," Spring 1998.

"Buck Ain't No Ordinary Dog" also was published in the column "Time Well Wasted" in the *Fayette Tribune* on July 24, 1997.